RIDE WITH ME

ALSO BY BRETT CHAMPAN

Rearview Sunset – A Novel

Fingerprints of God – Taking a Closer Look

RIDE WITH ME

Brett Champan

BRETT CHAMPAN

NorthWaters
PRESS

Northwoods • Chicago

Copyright © 2016 by Brett Champan

All rights reserved. No portion of this book may be reproduced, stored in a retrieval system, or transmitted in any form or by any means—electronic, mechanical, photocopy, recording, scanning, or other—except for brief quotations in critical reviews or articles, without the prior written permission of the publisher.

Published by NorthWaters Press

ISBN: 978-0-9883321-2-6

Printed in the United States of America

To the giver of breath and purpose who watches over us in all seasons.

And to those in my life who seek to stand on the higher ground,

And serve something greater than themselves.

May we continue to ride hard and breathe deep all our days to come.

A Note from the Author

Dear Reader,

RIDE WITH ME began to unfold in the spring of 2011, but its true inception dates to a couple years earlier when I wrote my first novel, REARVIEW SUNSET. In that story, young Beau Jamison had a wise old friend named Earl, and Earl attached himself to many readers. In light of this, I wanted to share Earl's story in greater detail.

So in the pages to come, you'll learn more about Earl and his journey with his wife, Ruth. Earl was a simple man with deep character who lived a full, adventurous life that refreshed many others. It wasn't always an easy life, but one marked by joy, commitment, and unwavering faith in something greater than himself.

And at the end of this story, you'll find a brief excerpt from REARVIEW SUNSET as well.

I hope you enjoy RIDE WITH ME, which is best read with hot coffee and a crackling fire nearby.

Yours,
Brett Champan

There is a time for everything, and a season for every activity under heaven.

The Teacher, Ecclesiastes 3:1

Prologue

September 19, 2000—Twilight reflections from the porch

I could feel the soft, cool breeze at my back, together with the fading rays of sun warming my face as Jessie and I sat out on the lake earlier tonight. I was lulled by the sounds of water lapping up against the sides of the canoe, and while some may argue that canines do not possess the capacity to revel in such pleasure, it appeared that she was too. She sat so still in the front, facing forward with her nose in the air and a look of pleasure on her face. Soon the light of day receded, replaced by twilight, which is now fading and giving way to a starry sky that will rival the beauty of the setting sun.

After all these years at this cabin and on this lake, and after so many seasons that have come and gone, I am still so thankful that the beauty of the sky has not grown normal to me nor dulled in my senses. It is one of the few things that remain unaltered while everything else changes so rapidly. Breathtaking skies and the creative hand that made them—two constants that I am most grateful for.

Tomorrow is a special day, and I know that anticipation for the morning will pierce me when I lay my head on the pillow tonight. I am a bit nervous, for I get steamrolled by emotions each year when going down this trail. I can go no other route, though, for I've learned that memory is one of man's greatest gifts and must be cultivated and exercised in order to keep it sharp.

One fine woman has often reminded me of this truth, especially when I have been down or disillusioned. "Babe, remember why you're doing what you're doing," she'd say, sometimes showing me a picture of a smiling child from the orphanage or reading an encouraging letter someone had sent us.

It is said that there is a time for everything, and a season for every activity on this earth. These words have intersected my path and fortified my course countless times, and they do once again as I sit here now, a day of remembrance almost upon me.

> To all the years that have passed,
>> Full of sweet times and memories that will forever last:
>
> I am again opening my door wide to you, despite my fears,
>> And I trust that you shall again bring more laughter and tears.
>
> Come, yesterday, come, for a time.

Shoebox Memories

The light sound of rain tapping on the roof gently woke Earl from his sleep. It was still dark outside, though he knew that dawn was drawing near. He lay still on his side facing the window, comforted by the falling raindrops and the blowing wind that amplified the peace of the early morning hour. These elements soothed him in ways he couldn't describe.

Just then he heard a bit of rustling coming from the floor next to his bed, and Jessie stood up and came into view. As usual, she rested her head on the bed, nuzzling her moist nose an inch from his and whining softly.

"Hey sweetheart," he said with a chuckle. "You never fail to pursue your morning lovin', do you?"

Earl reached over toward the nightstand and turned on the small, dark wooden lamp and began petting the yellow Labrador, whose big brown eyes looked so earnestly into his. "Always so loyal and kind." Jessie was now nine years old—though still in excellent health. Earl attributed this to a life full of walks and runs in the woods, frequent interaction with other humans and dogs, a good diet, and most of all, plenty of belly rubs.

As Jessie pressed in closer, Earl finally gave in and patted the mattress a few times. This was a regular practice nowadays, but despite the frequency it always felt like a treat to them both. She knew exactly what he was saying, and in an instant she had bound up onto the bed and nuzzled her back into his chest, pushing her paws into the bed in order to get as close as possible.

"You are something," he said, grinning with delight while her head rested just underneath his chin, his arm resting over the top of her body. "You know the missus wouldn't approve of this, though I bet she'd have a hard time resisting you too." Jessie wasn't allowed in the bed, at least not every day, until Earl began sleeping alone again. Though his wife had loved the dog and sometimes invited her up, she had also enjoyed having the bed to themselves. And Earl's desire to please her had exceeded all else, including his love for his dog.

Earl eventually decided it was time to rise, and sat up and swung his legs onto the floor. Looking out the window he could see a hint of pink on the horizon, and it quickened his spirit as it always did. He put on his robe, then knelt beside the bed to pray, giving thanks for all things. At the forefront of his list was that special autumn day many years ago, when he stood under the golden maples and slipped a ring onto the finger of a beautiful young woman who had so effortlessly captured his heart.

"Amen," he whispered, then rose to his feet and made for the shower. Jessie looked attentively at her master, motionless other than the licking of her chops and the slight wagging of her tail, exhibiting no desire to get off the soft, plush bed.

"It's a special day, girl. Go ahead and lie there a little longer."

After showering, Earl put on a pair of blue jeans, a cotton T-shirt, an old flannel, and a pair of slippers, then walked downstairs with Jessie following close behind. As was his custom, he went straight to the kitchen and began brewing a pot of strong coffee. Earl avoided drinking it throughout the whole day as he felt like it interfered with his ability to possess a clear mind. But in the morning, he liked his coffee to have guts. He was a man of zest, and he felt that his drink should have zest too.

After pressing the button for the machine to start brewing, he walked to the front door and began putting on his shoes. Jessie was again following close, and began whining softly while looking into his eyes and then at the door. She knew that it was time for their morning walk, and she loved being outside as much as he did.

"Let's go, girl!" he said after tying his shoes and opening the door. She bolted out of the cabin with a speed that defied her age.

There was a fine trail that led through the forest, and that was the route they took this morning. Jessie sprang out in front and dashed into the woods, here and there and all over, occasionally coming back to make sure Earl was doing okay before bounding back into the forest with her nose close to the earth, picking up scents.

The clouds were clearing and it was turning out to be a beautiful day, accentuated by a cool, brisk air that enlivened their senses. Earl walked along the well-worn path that led up and down small hills and ravines, through dense forest and sometimes mossy earth that was covered by a canopy of large oak and maple trees with patches of white birch and aspen. The forest was a brilliant showcase of deep green, bright yellow, and radiant orange. Along the way there was a small creek that Earl could rarely resist stopping to admire. The relaxing sight and sound of water trickling over the rocks and the soothing motion of the current held him in awe.

The trail eventually led to a gravel road that the two walked down a short ways before turning around and heading for home. With breakfast waiting, their pace quickened.

Earl ate eggs and toast with a generous portion of all-natural peanut butter that he bought from the country store and a more moderate portion of homemade strawberry jam. He would prefer to pour half of the jar onto his toast, but the jam, a gift from his daughter, was special to him, and he wanted it to last as long as possible. He then poured a cup of coffee and headed for the porch, picking up his journal and his small black leather Bible along the way.

He also picked up a weathered cardboard shoebox from the small desk by the door. On the lid was a picture of him in earlier years. He was sitting in front of a lake with a beautiful woman by his side. Earl's arm was wrapped around her, and behind them a beautiful evening sky boasted a stunning sunset that set the horizon on fire.

Of all material objects on this earth, this shoebox was his most cherished possession.

Earl walked to the old wooden rocker that his grandfather had made for his grandma and slowly sat down after setting the box and coffee cup on the small wood table at the chair's side. He enjoyed the subtle creaking sound that the chair made on the wood when he rocked, and laughed when recalling how his brother would rock so hard and fast on those recliners when growing up that they had been retired into firewood long before they were intended to.

He eventually picked up his Bible and opened it to the book of Ecclesiastes. Normally he read Proverbs each morning, but Ecclesiastes felt fitting for this particular day. He then picked up his cup and began to read, slowly, stopping every once in a while to let the words absorb into his soul. Like fine chocolate or a fresh cut of steak, he believed these words should not be consumed too quickly.

After reading, he set the book down on the floor next to him, picked up his journal and captured a few of his thoughts onto paper before setting it down again and slowly picking up the shoebox, which he placed gently on his lap. He ran his hand over it a few times to clear off a small amount of dust, then placed his hand on the edge of the lid to open it when his eyes were drawn to the woods in front of him by the sounds of a songbird. The morning sun had just begun to break through the trees as well. Frozen by the sight and sounds, he stared into the distance, reminded that he was anything but alone.

"Amazing," he whispered softly to himself, silently marveling at the magnificence of the creation before him, and how, after all these years, there still existed those wonderful, though ever-so-fleeting moments where he was so deeply moved. In his earlier years he had a difficult time seeing the beauty in life, blinded by to-do lists, outside pressures, and the brokenness of the world around him—so consumed by life's complexities that he just could not see. Over time, he learned the secret of looking beyond the mire and paradoxes, and he longed to help others see it too.

When he finally returned his gaze to the small shoebox, it was with a deep breath.

He opened the lid, and there, just as it always had been, were two stacks of letters held together by twine. Sitting atop the first stack was a letter that began "To Earl, my loyal husband and best friend."

Earl pulled out the letter, took a long look at it, and carefully reached for his mug and took another sip of coffee. A couple years ago he had accidently spilled a few drops on the letter and would have kicked himself for doing so, if he hadn't known that she would laugh at it, since he had always taken lightly her suggestions to be careful with his coffee. He loathed coming home with coffee-stained clothes, which she never failed to clean for him.

"Another spill, honey?" she would say with a grin. One year, he finally broke down and bought one of those expensive coffee mugs with a lid on it for when he and Jessie drove in the Jeep.

Earl smiled, looking at the stain on the letter almost with a sense of gratefulness for the priceless memory it produced. Then, with another deep breath and an adjustment in his seat, he gently opened the letter and began to read.

Dear Earl,

It is a strange thing to begin writing a letter to one you love so deeply, knowing that it may not be read until after you have flown away. Up until now I could not have imagined having the strength of heart to do this, though it seems we are often granted the power to do extraordinary things when we have to. This appears to be one of those times.

You may not notice anything special about this shoebox, though it is special to me. Aside from the appreciation you always had for these small cardboard constructions, which you found useful for so many purposes, there was a time when you bought me a new pair of shoes that you knew I wanted, and commented that you could hardly wait for all the walks that we had yet to share with each other. I always felt so loved when you said things like that, though for some reason those words, at that moment, captivated me. I was so eager to go for a walk with you in those new shoes that day, and I determined to save that box for something special. I'm not sure if you noticed it missing for a while, though if you did, now you know where it went.

And now, in this hour, I can think of nothing more special to have saved it for.

In this small shoebox you will find the letters we wrote over the years, along with excerpts from our journals that create a portrait of the life we spent together, especially our early years. Stephanie helped photocopy them; I originally considered cutting them out, but I just couldn't bring myself to physically alter the pages.

Should these be our final days, I wanted to leave you with something to remember me by, something to spark your already sharp memory of all that we held dear over the years. Those golden maples especially come to mind.

I am reminded of them now as I look at the trees outside the window of this hospital room. They are beautiful—almost as beautiful as those we know so well. Some days they sway with such force that I wonder if they will be uprooted and crash to the ground, though I know their roots are strong, and though they may lose a branch or two, they will hold. Other days they are incredibly still and stately, and if it weren't for the occasional breeze that makes a few of their leaves quiver, I would think I'm looking at a painting. I can just stare at those trees for so long, and in a way that I know you understand, it brings me peace.

Today, their leaves are golden and red, and beyond them the sky is such a deep blue and the clouds so puffy and white. Soon, though, winter will come like a thief in the night, and the leaves will fall to the ground . . .

I have more to write, my love, and you will find the rest of my words in an envelope on the bottom of the stack. I ask that you read it last, though, and I hope the journey that leads to it warms your heart as much as it did my own.

I love you,
Ruth

Earl looked up from the letter and gazed out beyond the porch. His body was still, with eyes fixed on a batch of golden maple trees that sat in the yard, radiant as pure gold drenched in sunlight. These trees, as well as the maples outside her room, were not the same ones that Ruth was referring to in her letter, though they were adored nonetheless, reminders of what was, what is, and what is still to come. He stared at them for a moment before returning his attention to the box in front of him.

His eyes now moist, he recalled the time when he first received the shoebox. He just stared at it all morning before opening it, knowing that, coming from Ruth, there was something powerful and poignant within that would leave him a changed person. He also recalled the first time he opened the shoebox and read this first letter. Overcome with emotion, he had to set it down and could not return to the box for weeks.

And with that, he rose slowly from his chair and went inside to replenish his cup of coffee. When he returned to the porch and slowly sat down again, he picked up the shoebox and withdrew the first letter from Ruth's stack.

"Happy anniversary, honey," he said, then slowly unfolded the letter that would usher him into days long passed.

Country Store Romance

May 5, 1942
From Ruth's journal

I met a handsome young man in an old country store this evening. To be completely honest, I was melted by his crooked, genuine smile and drawn to his eyes that were lit by a touch of fire. He also had what I perceived to be an unusual dose of humility for one his age. I know I may never see him again, but if we are to return here, I cannot deny that hope is within me.

May 5, 1942
From Earl's journal

I'm not sure that I ever truly stopped breathing, even for a moment, when meeting a girl—until today. Her name is Ruth, and the only thing more beautiful than her physical appearance was her spirit that flooded the country store where I met her. Her eyes were deep and exuded life, and she possessed such a soft and sweet demeanor. Yet she was also strong and steady in a quiet, gentle way. God, I know you don't look more highly upon man based on what he does, but I have to say that I'd do just about anything if you bring her back this way.

"Earl, let's go! Mother needs a few ingredients for dinner and it's getting late in the day. You can work on your fly rod later."

"Just one more second," replied Earl. He was tying a tippet that required considerable concentration, and didn't want to be bothered at that moment.

"Come on! The longer it takes us, the longer dinner will push into the evening and that means less fishing time."

Earl stopped and looked up. "Okay," he replied, this time very much in tune with his brother's thinking. "I'm comin'!"

Earl set the pieces of the fly rod down in an orderly way, then jumped to his feet and made for the door. The post-dinner fishing outings were a treasured occasion for the guys in the family, whether fly-fishing in the river or on the lake in the boat, and Earl did not want to let anything under his power ruin it, especially on a beautiful late spring day like today. With partly cloudy skies that allowed intervals of sunlight to peek through and pleasant temperatures that climbed into the upper fifties after a few very brisk days, the conditions were ripe for a good evening of fishing.

The two brothers ran out of the family room and battled to get out the door first—just like they did while growing up. Tom now lived in his own house in Cringle, a nearby town less than a half-hour away, but he visited his family often—especially for meals. Earl, now twenty-one, still lived with his parents, though only temporarily. Having recently purchased a place of his own not far from Tom's, he continued to live with his parents while restoring the old house on his property.

This time, Tom gained the upper hand and jammed Earl into the frame, squishing his face into the wood. They proceeded to scramble into Tom's Chevy pickup, Tom turning the key and firing up the big, faithful engine.

"Danny! Come on boy!" yelled Earl, calling out for his friend. Moments later, Earl's dog, half yellow lab and half golden retriever, came bolting around the corner of the house, running with everything he had toward the truck. A look of pure joy and exhilaration was upon his face, his eyes open wide while his jowls flapped wildly. He wore what appeared to be a smile as he leaped effortlessly into the bed of the truck, sticking his head into the cab window to say hello.

Danny had been given to Earl just a couple years earlier, a gift from a family that was moving and couldn't take the dog with them. They knew that Earl was looking for a dog, and Danny proved a perfect fit. He bonded with his new master instantly, never letting him out of his sight. Most nights Danny even slept on Earl's bed.

Good ol' Danny loved road trips, and it didn't matter if it was twenty minutes to the store or hours to another county. Most of the time he would sit inside the truck, upright just like Earl. However, if he was tired or just craving some snuggling, he would lie down and rest his head on the nearest lap, sometimes alternating from driver to passenger.

Meanwhile, their father sat inside on the recliner after a long day's work. He paused from preparing his own fishing pole to watch them from the front window. He loved the sight of his boys and the dog so full of energy and vigor.

"Those two boys are a wonderful sight, honey. They possess so much zeal for life," he said with a chuckle to his wife, who was in the kitchen preparing dinner.

"And you know where they get that zeal from, don't you," she said lovingly as she walked towards him, leaned down slowly and kissed his cheek, and then, unexpectedly, caressed his face with a handful of mashed potatoes that she was preparing.

"Yes, I suppose I—hey!" he yelled when realizing what she had done. With a face covered in what looked like shaving cream, Richard leaped out of his chair and began chasing her around the kitchen, captivated by the mischievous grin on her face. He chased her around the table for a minute before he caught her in an embrace and gave her a big mashed potato kiss.

The Chevy rolled down the gravel driveway and onto the road, wind racing in through the windows while Tom and Earl talked about fishing and what parts of the river they would go to that evening. Only years later would they realize that the thrill had been less the fishing and more the simple joy of uninterrupted camaraderie.

The twenty-minute drive passed quickly, and soon they pulled onto the gravel lot of the old country store.

"We'll be right back Danny. You stay and guard the truck, okay boy?" said Earl from the side of the vehicle. He always had a hard time leaving the creature, even if only for a few minutes. Danny stayed in the truck, peering back with sad, understanding eyes.

As they walked into the store, they were greeted by Mrs. Burke, who always had a way of making them feel special. She was arranging cans of soup on a shelf, and her husband, with whom she ran the store, was behind the counter. The boys proceeded towards the aisles, picked up the ingredients and went to the checkout counter. In front of them was what appeared to be a husband and wife with their two children—a young son and a lovely daughter in a dress with long auburn hair.

Mountain was a small town where limited amounts of new activity, and the two boys wondered silently who these people were. Perhaps they were tourists just passing through, or newcomers to their hometown. Regardless, they seemed like a warm, respectable family judging by the conversation they were sharing with Mr. Burke, and Earl could not help but be a little curious about the identity of this young lady with beautiful flowing hair and slender figure. That was all he could see of her, though he had already determined to get a glimpse of her face before they left.

Unknowingly, perhaps, Mr. Burke gave him a hand in his endeavor.

"Ah, and here are two of the finest young men in the county. Meet the Timmings boys; sons of my dear friends Richard and Patricia," said Mr. Burke while motioning his guests to look behind them.

The family turned around and cordially greeted the two rugged young men who felt caught off guard, both by the unexpected introduction and by the well-dressed family. Earl felt his face flush with a touch of embarrassment because of his worn, almost shabby clothes. But his embarrassment didn't have time to linger, for Mr. Burke had already begun to introduce the family.

"Young men, meet the Benson family. They are fine folks who may be relocating to our town soon."

The family greeted Tom and Earl, and the warmth and sincerity they radiated struck the boys head-on and broke down any uneasiness they felt.

Furthermore, it was at this moment when Earl was hooked by the girl with long, flowing hair who stood facing him. The sight of her lovely eyes and sweet smile melted him.

As their eyes briefly met, a subtle, reserved smile crept across each of their faces. Earl did his best to stay composed and welcoming towards the parents, though despite his best efforts, it was obvious to everyone but himself that his attention was hijacked by this young lady, who did a better job of concealing her own interest.

"Steven. A pleasure to meet you two," said the father, in a warm tone that hid his watchful and appraising eye. He was a good judge of character and could see something in Earl that kept him from entertaining the notion of shooting the young buck in his rear end with a shotgun after kicking him out of the front door. Steven proceeded to give them each a warm handshake and went on to introduce the names of his wife and daughter.

"Pleasure to meet you as well," said Earl, looking last at the daughter, who was introduced as Ruth. He could feel his heart pound within his chest, and hoped that no one could hear it.

"Well, Mr. Burke, Tom, and Earl, we'd best be on our way," said Steven after a few more minutes of conversation. "Perhaps we will see you all again soon."

"I do hope so, Mr. Benson. The town of Mountain would be honored to have you join its ranks," replied Mr. Burke.

The family departed the store, though as they were leaving, Ruth turned her head around one last time, where her eyes connected with Earl's.

And then she was gone.

The two boys paid for their items and chatted a bit more with Mr. Burke before departing. They discovered the family was visiting from Iowa and may be returning, for good, if Steven accepted an executive position with a nearby lumber company that a friend of his worked for.

Tom and Earl exited the store and placed the items in the pickup, smothered Danny with some affection, and set out for home. Tom was again behind the wheel, while Earl sat looking intently out the window into the soft blue sky. Tom, ever perceiving, had noticed the exchange between his brother and the young woman and wasted little time before commenting on it.

"Well, brother, I honestly thought your eyes were going to shoot out of your head in there."

"What do you mean?" asked Earl in a mildly defensive tone.

"Don't give me that. That girl just made you forget your own name."

"I don't know about that."

"Come on now, don't try foolin' me!"

"Well, she sure was pretty. And those eyes, and her voice . . ." replied Earl, leaning his head back.

"You are smitten, my brother, no doubt about it. In a matter of minutes, you have been smitten!" Tom said, enjoying the sight of his brother trying to cover up his blissful state and appear unaltered. Earl had little to say in return and continued looking at the sky that passed by, his arm hanging out the window to catch the warm summer air.

"Okay, maybe a little."

Tom smiled and looked over at Earl, and saying nothing more, began humming a tune while looking out ahead from behind the wheel. He knew Earl's keen sense of discernment of others and how seriously he took the admonition from his father to guard his heart, and this made Tom all the more curious of what would become of the country store encounter he had just witnessed.

"Thank you for this meal, for this family, and for always providing for us. Please keep us safe, and close. And may you continue to watch over those young men serving overseas. Amen." Richard's prayer was followed by a pause and an *Amen* from Patricia, his sons, and little Stephanie, the youngest. They were all aware that this word did not represent the end of a prayer, but rather an agreement with the words just spoken, and they were all truly in agreement of the goodness of food and family that they were about to enjoy.

With the exception of Stephanie, who was too young to comprehend the situation, they were also in agreement on the need to pray for the military. World War II had begun just four months earlier in December with the bombing of Pearl Harbor by Japan, who together with Germany and Italy, declared war on the United States. And while their daily routines continued, the war was always on their minds.

With golden rays of sunlight bursting through the trees, passing through the dining room windows and finally onto the dinner table, the family began to fill their plates and robust conversation and laughter filled the room. The young men were energized by thoughts of fishing, keeping one eye on the skies the whole time. There was a dark row of clouds coming down from the northwest that could threaten their outing.

"Only heavy thunder and lightning will turn us away, boys," said Richard reassuringly, noticing their looks of consternation while peering at the skies. "And it doesn't look like those clouds have that in store for us. I bet they break up before they even get here." He went quiet for a moment then spoke again before taking his first bite. "Patricia, this meal looks wonderful."

"I agree," said Tom as he shoveled a large portion of mashed potatoes onto his plate. Earl and little Stephanie nodded in agreement.

"Well, you'd better taste it first before complimenting me too much," said Patricia with an air of confidence and proud smile that she was doing her best to conceal. She was quite sure that this meal of venison burgers complete with potatoes, grilled asparagus, and her special cherry brownies would succeed in satisfying them. It always had in the past.

Richard took a large bite of the burger and let out a gentle moan as he slowly chewed, smiling with his eyes closed. Stephanie started to giggle. Patricia's smile grew, beaming inside from her husband's reaction. She wondered silently to herself how after all these meals and all the positive responses her family voiced towards her cooking, it still felt so good to see them enjoy themselves once again. She reasoned that seeing those she loved so much in a state of satisfaction was something that could never grow old.

Their children grinned while eating, more impacted by the loving gestures that were taking place between their parents than the food itself.

The simple enjoyment they were all experiencing made the two parents glow inside. These conversations and all their transparency were not just natural by-products of living under that same roof for so long, but were the fruit of engaging their children through all the years. And there was an undeniable power and blessing that came from simply sitting around the dinner table on a consistent basis regardless of how busy life could be.

In their commitment to cultivating a home of openness and love, Richard and Patricia frequently had to remind themselves of where they had come from. Life had not always been this full of joy and security.

In their early years of marriage, Richard tended to lean too heavily on the bottle in tough times. He became rough with his wife more than once. His abuse was mostly verbal, though there were a few times where words turned into a shove, and shove into deep regret. Richard was a respected man in town—a hard worker, a provider, and leader for his family and community, and an advocate for those in need. Yet he had his weaknesses, not seen by many, and possessed little control over his anger and depression and would occasionally lose his cool in very big and painful ways.

The children were very young at the time and with the exception of Tom, the eldest, had been oblivious to most of this, though through stories and what recollection they did have of those years, they too knew that life had changed.

Tom had been exposed to a few more of his father's outbursts and a couple of times even had a showdown with him in an effort to protect his mother. One time in particular, Richard had Tom up against the wall after an argument, and the situation was looking to get even worse. Both had their fists clenched, ready to swing, until the sound of Patricia's voice crying out pierced the room and made them both freeze in shock. In an instant, the flame in their eyes receded and their arms dropped, pulled down with the weight of shame and regret.

For some time after that, Tom had a hard time looking at his dad without a burning anger hiding behind his eyes.

However, change was in store for the Timmings—change that would be ushered in by one of the leaders from a church in a nearby town who kept knocking on their front door at seemingly random, yet mysteriously fitting times. They had visited this church once in the past and had briefly met him, and for that reason alone they gave him a little of their attention. But on more than a couple occasions, they would hear the knock. It would come when they were in the midst of an argument that was growing out of control, or when Richard was tempted to carry his frustration down to the local tavern, or when Patricia was silently wishing for a way out of the marriage, both of them shocked and ashamed for even entertaining such thoughts.

"Mr. and Mrs. Timmings, it's Ed again. I just wanted to remind you that if there is anything I can do for you or anything you'd like to talk about . . ." They had heard this on several occasions, wide-eyed and dumbfounded at both the sincerity and quiet strength of this man and the impossible timing of his arrivals. Each time they would decline his help and send him away, then retire to their individual toiling, the flames of their rage now reduced to embers.

But on one occasion, when the kids were way and the two were in the midst of a barn-burning argument that seemed to have no end in sight, Richard, to the great surprise of Patricia, invited the man inside to talk. As soon as they sat down at the table with coffee in hand, he began asking Ed all sorts of questions about God and heaven and everything in between. The man spoke winsomely yet pointedly, easily and rapidly quoting scripture as if he had just eaten the Bible, sharing words that were alive and relevant to human life—

something neither Richard nor Patricia were accustomed to with their religious backgrounds.

Over the coming months, the man stopped coming unannounced, for Richard had started to invite him over. During this time, Richard's heart churned and began to soften at the thought of a relationship with the Creator of all things, a God who began to reveal himself as a loving father rather than a hammer in the sky, a Being whom Richard always knew was there but couldn't understand and therefore resented. And that this relationship came through a son who had been a carpenter, and not via any earthly priest or good works, was both comforting and thrilling to him.

Unknown to Richard, Patricia's heart had already yielded and embraced this man's message weeks before, and when she saw her husband do the same, there was no small amount of tears that flowed at the dinner table that night.

A new chapter was about to begin in the Timmings household, one that would impact generations to come and allow light to pour into that humble house in Mountain.

Richard still had some rough edges, but for those who knew him well, the change was nothing short of remarkable. And it was a change that sent ripples through the entire family, including Earl. It made an impression that would stay with him throughout all the days of his life.

Now there were times at the dinner table where he saw his mother look at his father so lovingly that his father's eyes got watery. In Richard's mind, he wondered how something so beautiful and sweet could look at him the way she did after all the years that he had treated her in a manner less fitting than she deserved. Sometimes he'd excuse himself from the table, saying he needed to get some air, though everyone knew that he was simply uncomfortable revealing his emotions and ineffective at holding them back. He'd go out on the porch for a moment and look into the horizon, asking for a reminder that his past was forgiven and for the grace to be this woman's loving husband as well as these children's caring father. After a few moments he would return to the table with a noticeably soft and kind demeanor, and all would be quiet for a few moments until Patricia would again break the silence with some aptly spoken words that prompted laughter and discussion.

There were a few rare times, however, where Richard would let his emotions pour out at the table.

On one of those occasions, he began to slide his chair out after the meal, though this time he stopped as tears began to flow from his eyes that looked pointedly at his wife. "I love you . . ." he said in a choked voice. He then looked at each of the kids, and with the same voice continued, "You are all beautiful, precious, strong, and cherished. I am so grateful and proud of you." Though he showed much love through his actions, he was not very good at expressing his love verbally, and these words penetrated the hearts of each of them. The sound of Patricia's sniffling could be heard as she sat with big watery eyes that were full of tenderness. "Take hands," said Richard with gentle authority. So with everyone connected, he prayed a prayer that came from the deepest caverns of his heart, full of power and passion, thanking God for his family and simply but earnestly requesting that they and generations to come would never take their eyes off of him. Earl would never forget seeing his father open up like that, and few things influenced him in his life like that night did.

And so it was at this same dinner table that such warmth flowed; a place where all could be themselves, accepted and listened to, even in their silence. And on this particular night, Earl's relative silence and preoccupation did not go unnoticed.

"Earl, you're awfully quiet and thoughtful tonight. Everything okay?" asked Patricia as everyone was scraping the last bits of cherry brownie off their plates.

"Yeah," he replied, "just thinking about the next project I need to start at the house. And looking forward to getting on the water tonight."

"Is that all, brother?" asked Tom with a slight grin after a few moments of debating whether he should speak up. As usual, he chose in favor of it. "Are you sure there is no one—I mean, nothing else that has captured your mind?"

Earl looked at him with a mixture of mild frustration and disbelief, shaking his head. But he couldn't hold back a grin either.

"Hmm . . . I see," said Patricia, slowly and deliberately leaning forward in her chair, placing her elbows on the table and resting her chin on her palms while looking directly at her son. "Who is she?" The fragrance of romance was something that Patricia could always detect, and she was capable of picking up a scent through the thickest of woods regardless of the season.

Richard, smiling softly, leaned forward as well, now fully engaged in the unfolding drama.

"It's probably nothing," Earl said in an attempt to calm the rising tide of interest. But it was no use. His family, including little Stephanie sitting next to him, were all fully aware of his sensibility and caution towards women, and they recognized that something real was happening. Earl's red face only confirmed it. "I met her at the country store. She is visiting town with her family and may move here if her dad gets a nearby job. Don't even know if I'll ever see her again."

"Well, there's nothing wrong with hoping," said Richard.

"No, nothing at all," agreed Patricia enthusiastically.

"Is she pretty?" asked Stephanie in her sweet voice. Earl wasn't in the mood to share any more. But with one look at his cute little wide-eyed, smiling sister, whose legs began anxiously dangling back and forth under the chair, causing her whole body to sway slightly, he couldn't help but soften.

"She is beautiful," he said after a deep breath, looking at Stephanie with a grin that covered his whole face. Then he stole a glance at the others, who were listening attentively, and rose from his seat to end the conversation.

"Well, I guess we'll see what's in store. But for now," said Richard as he rose from his seat, "it's time to go fishing." His words, wisely chosen and appreciated by his younger son, signaled the end of dinner and the beginning of the Timmings boys' most sought-after adventures.

The three men quickly gathered their gear and set out, Danny bouncing beside them with pride and excitement. He saw the fishing poles and knew exactly where they were going.

They climbed into the truck and drove down an old gravel road to one of their favorite spots along the river. Each of the men looked into the sky more than once as they traversed the trail through the woods, noting the clouds that continued to grow in dominance. Yet time remained to fish. And after putting on their waders and stepping into the water, fish they did. Occasionally there were short spurts of conversation, but most of the time the sound of the river was the only thing to be heard. The men were left to themselves to ponder life, secure and content in the knowledge that loved ones were close.

"Hey, did you guys hear that Philip left for basic training yesterday?" asked Earl, breaking the silence. Philip was a coworker of Earl's whom he had known for many years.

"Yeah, I just heard that," replied Tom. "He—"

"Ah, no sense in talking about that tonight boys," said his father, who feigned uninterest in the topic and waded upstream a bit. "Tonight, we just fish and enjoy this river." He knew his two boys were considering enlisting—if the draft didn't find them first—and he just wasn't ready for the thought of them being pulled into the war's current.

Tom and Earl looked at one another. They knew their father's heart, and out of respect, they changed the subject and waded upstream as well.

The whole time, Danny patrolled the shoreline, keeping his humans in sight while digging holes and pursuing squirrels, chipmunks, and any other amusement the land had to offer, including dead fish that had washed ashore. He would roll around in the rotting fish if his master's eyes were directed elsewhere.

And there was no telling how many times Danny got away with it before Earl finally caught him in the act.

"Danny! Get out of there!" Danny shot up like a bullet and looked right at Earl, ears down. He knew he had done wrong, but he just couldn't help himself.

"Ha!" laughed Tom. "Looks like Danny found his treasure. We're going to have a smelly ride home tonight fellas!"

"Good grief, boys. You're going to scare away all the fish!" whispered his father hoarsely while laughing himself.

After the drama of Danny's fish-roll ended, Earl returned to the thoughtful state he had been in all night, and Richard and Tom couldn't help but notice. But they weren't surprised, aware as they both were of the mystery of how a girl can affect a man's entire being and kindle a fire deep within the soul.

Earl hoped to see Ruth again, and was wrestling within himself over not letting this hope get too high. Earl was a dreamer of sorts—not an undisciplined chaser of fantasies but a young man of vision and of sensitivity to the deep things of life and the possibilities within each day. And one of those deep things happened to be romance. He was aware that some people felt God was unconcerned and separated from such an idea, though he wondered how they ever came to such a shallow, misdirected conclusion. After all, Isaac was hooked by Rebecca, Jacob smitten by Rachel, and Boaz captivated by young Ruth. Therefore,

Earl reasoned that there was something absolutely genuine, real, and pure about this mysterious power displayed between a male and female.

The men fished on until darkness began to set in, and with the sky still filled with a mixture of serene, starry blue skies and ominous dark clouds that were now passing out of range, they packed up their gear, as well as the rainbow trout and smallmouth bass they caught, and set out for home. Relaxed and contented, they continued to enjoy the camaraderie while talking of the night's catch and those that had escaped.

As they drove along, Richard again reveled in the conversation with his two sons, thinking to himself of the journey that led him and his family to this day. He was blown away by the thought of how quickly the years have passed and how much they contained. He had made a decision, years ago, to leave the city and risk the challenges of rural living, and on this day, as much as ever, he had no regrets.

And his younger son would soon be especially thankful for the decision as well.

Sweet Rays of Light

May 23, 1942
From Ruth's journal

Father got the job! We just returned days ago to this charming small town in northern Wisconsin, which is now our new home. My heart still aches with the goodbyes that were said in Iowa—to dear friends who I just graduated high school with, and many other loved ones that I may never see again. However, I know the ache will eventually pass like the melting snow in springtime. And thankfully the memories, as well as some of those friendships, will remain. I shall always treasure them.

Tomorrow we will be going to a church that the store owner invited us to. We've been told it is full of life and some wonderful people. I am truly excited.

And, just maybe, I'll see him there.

It was a gray Sunday morning as rain fell softly down on Mountain. Households throughout the county were lulled into tranquility by the light tapping of raindrops hitting the roof and the wind moving softly through the trees. The Timmings were among those who woke to these sounds and all decided, without consulting each other, to remain under the covers a bit longer.

Eventually they rose and began to prepare for church before sitting down for a quick breakfast of eggs, toast, orange juice, and coffee.

As soon as the last yolk was soaked up with the last bit of toast, they piled out of the house and into the Plymouth, driving off down the gravel road that commenced the half-hour drive. They passed endless fields and winding forest roads that invited their gaze and evoked daydreams of all sorts. Though they had traveled this road countless times, it somehow never lost its magic.

Soon they arrived to the small community church, which was perched on high-level ground and overlooked a great valley that was fittingly referred to as Sunset Valley, for it had a way of capturing some of the most beautiful sunsets around. A river ran through the valley, and like the sunsets, it had a reputation for stealing second glances from all who looked in its direction. And on this particular morning, Earl was one of those who could not help but look as he and his family walked briskly through the moist air towards the church.

The building, constructed of wood and stone, was a delight to the eyes. Though humble and relatively unadorned, it had been built with great care and precision by local builders who had themselves been members of the church. Local families had also contributed to the landscaping, which included a mix of wildflowers, maple trees, and lush, well-groomed grass. Though the congregation knew that it was only a building and plot of land, and that God's presence was not confined to brick and mortar, it had desired to make the place resemble a small slice of heaven's beauty on earth, and over the years it had succeeded in doing so.

The Timmings entered the building and visited with a few people before sitting in one of the pews. Soon the choir started, and those listening began to sing along with voices that filled the dark-stained wood sanctuary and burst through the windows into the surrounding forest. When the choir had finished, a woman began playing the piano with great skill, and she sang with a voice that was equally beautiful. As she sang, rays of bright white sunlight began to break through the clouds and beam in through the windows, creating a warm glow that Earl believed was quite fitting for the moment.

Earl loved the piano, always had. He loved the way the sounds moved him in ways he was unable to articulate. He sat in reverence, engulfed in a deep peace that filled the sanctuary.

At one point he began looking around at all the different people, noticing their varied emotions. Peace, release, joy, but also regret, worry, and fear—it was all there. He wondered what was going on within their minds and hearts, knowing full well that some were dancing inside, some were crying, and some were dead.

As his eyes continued to travel around the sanctuary, they fell upon something that would hold his attention and refuse to let go. As he looked closer, he realized that he had beheld this sight once in the past, and now it caused his mind to wander from the glories and power of heaven and settle on the beauty of life on earth. It was Ruth, the girl from the country store. She sat with her family in a pew towards the front of the sanctuary on the other side of the aisle, and he wondered how it took him this long to notice her.

Earl took a deep breath and did his best to stay composed, though it was no easy task. He felt an energy run through him and his heart beat wildly in his chest.

"I was wondering when you were going to notice," whispered Tom with a grin, leaning over to speak into his ears.

"Has she been here the whole time?" asked Earl in a whisper.

"Yep," Tom replied, "and she even turned back to look at you once, but you were too caught up in your daydreaming to notice."

Earl began looking forward to the end of the service, which was an unfamiliar feeling. The pastor eventually came to the front and began to speak, and though he was a gifted orator with a humble, engaging personality, Earl had a difficult time focusing on anything he was saying. Thankfully, he reasoned to himself, words have a way of settling on hearts even when they initially fall on deaf ears. He stole a few more glances her way, again admiring her physical attractiveness and the beauty that radiated from her countenance. Even when sitting still, she seemed to exude warmth, peace, and sincerity.

At one point, she dipped her head down slightly, then looked back in Earl's direction. Their eyes met. Earl gently held her gaze for a moment before she smiled coyly and returned her attention to the front. His heart pounded all the harder, and at that moment he knew beyond a shadow of doubt that he had stumbled upon something very special and was determined to pursue this fine young lady with every ounce of courage he possessed.

After what seemed like an eternity to Earl, the service finally ended and everyone rose from their seats and began to talk with one another. Ruth stood in the front near her family, engaged in conversation with others who were introducing themselves for the first time. Earl spoke with a few people in the pew in front of him, but in spite of all his efforts at sincerity, he barely heard what they said. His mind was elsewhere. Then Ruth looked back in his direction, and he knew then that he had to make his way to her.

"Go on!" whispered Tom as he prodded his brother into the aisle with his elbow. Annoyed, Earl felt like punching him, but he decided against it to avoid making a scene.

Instead, he wisely channeled his frustration towards the task at hand, and with another deep breath he took the first step forward towards the great unknown.

He approached Ruth cordially, not wanting to burst into her conversation with an older woman. Once the woman saw him approach, though, she smiled warmly and excused herself. Ruth, who was very aware of Earl's approach, turned to face him and smiled warmly.

"Hi, Ruth," he began, certain his voice had betrayed the nervousness he was feeling. "I met you briefly at the country store a few weeks back. You were there with your family and I was . . ."

"I remember," said Ruth kindly, her voice putting him at ease. "You're Earl."

"Yes, I am," he responded, thankful that she remembered. "It is a pleasure to meet you again."

"Likewise," she responded, impressed at how well he could clean up when recalling his rugged appearance at the country store.

"So, is Mountain your new home now?" he continued.

"Yes it is," she replied, surprised at how comfortable she felt talking to him. "I do miss our old home and friends in Iowa, but it has been wonderful here so far."

Earl, doing his best to conceal his thrill over the news, was about to continue when Ruth's father approached. He looked at Earl with a warm smile and extended his arm, giving him a firm handshake.

"Good to meet you again, young man. We sure appreciate how welcoming you and the residents of Mountain have been to us."

"Thank you, sir. We're glad to have you here," Earl said humbly. He could sense the deep adoration this man had for his daughter.

"The Harmon family invited us to their place for a picnic later this afternoon. Hopefully we'll see you there. Ruth, we'll be out in the car waiting. Don't be long," he said gently, smiling at the both of them before turning and walking towards the door.

"Okay Dad, I'll be right there," said Ruth right before Mr. Benson turned away. She then turned her attention back to Earl. "I should be going. Will I see you at the picnic later?"

"Yes, you will," Earl assured her.

"Good," she responded with a hint of excitement.

Earl initiated their walk towards the door where his family was still talking with some others, and he said goodbye as she walked out the door. That Earl was walking along with a young woman did not go unnoticed by his family, whose faces revealed both curiosity and approval.

"Well?" asked Tom inquisitively while sitting next to him on the drive home.

"We're going to a picnic."

Earl and Tom quit fishing early that afternoon in order to leave for the picnic. After climbing into the truck and setting out, Tom again made it a point to remind Earl that there were no worthy, legitimate reasons under the sun to quit fishing early, especially on the Lord's Day—other than for a woman. Tom had a serious girlfriend of his own, and therefore had learned, oftentimes the hard way, the delicate balance between women and fishing. Earl, who actually wanted to leave even earlier, concurred and thanked his older brother for understanding.

They arrived just after three o'clock, well after most of the other guests, though the festivities were still in full swing. They parked the truck on the gravel drive and began walking along the fence line towards the picnic tables in the front yard, where they reunited with their own family and some other friends. The Harmons' property was a perfect place to gather for a picnic, with a huge yard that sat in between a forest and vast rolling fields. They were a large, gracious family who made a living off ranching and farming, and they loved to host.

It didn't take long for Earl to catch sight of Ruth's family, and after saying hello to a few people he made his way over to their table. However, he did not see Ruth anywhere. After a short while of doing his best to not appear distracted by Ruth's absence, Earl was relieved by Cynthia Benson, Ruth's mother, who had read his face twice over and graciously informed him that she had just gone off with some of the younger women to the stables and were likely out on a ride.

Cynthia also hinted that Ruth was looking forward to seeing him, though was unsure of when he'd arrive and did not want to miss out on the chance to go riding. Encouraged, Earl acknowledged that there were few better places that she could be than on horseback. He then accepted an invitation to a game of horseshoes with her father and some other men. He enjoyed the men's company, but his game was a little off; he had one eye on the path to the stables.

The afternoon passed quickly, and with its departure came the sweet, soft air of early evening that could lull even the most anxious person into a state of half-consciousness. This seemed evident as the pace of the gathering slightly subsided, with more people lingering at picnic tables and lawn chairs, caught up in deeper, quieter conversations, many of which centered around the latest news about the war. The wind moved softly through the trees, causing the leaves to gently flutter and sway. The clouds from the morning had passed, and the sun continued to warm the skin as it retired into the west.

By this time, Earl's desire to see Ruth had reached its summit, and he cordially excused himself and set out for the stables. He was also looking forward to some time away from the crowd, for despite his love of the fellowship and energy—

the children playing and laughing, the adults reconnecting and sharing stories—he needed to get away and recharge his own introverted soul. Spending time among these animals had always been one of the best ways for him to achieve this.

Arriving, he found the place quiet and serene. He walked onto the wooden porch that separated the building from the hitching posts, relishing the pounding and creaking sounds the planks made under each step of his boots. He was no stranger to these particular stables, or to the sights, sounds, and smells unique to the place that always made him feel right at home.

Earl had been a regular visitor to the Harmon's for years. He had helped them start a few of the horses and assisted them with random projects. In return, he was gifted one of the horses—a sorrel Kentucky Mountain named Obie, short for Obediah—and allowed to board it for free, as well as to come and go as he pleased.

The majority of the area around the stables was wooded, with small clearings mixed in. He stepped off the porch and walked around the rectangular hitching post, then leisurely walked back to the porch and leaned against the wood guardrail. He looked out at the herd that grazed there.

After a few minutes of observing the creatures, who were also passively observing him, one of them lifted his head, looked him square on, and gingerly began walking towards him. It was Obie. Earl always found it a thrill when one of these large animals initiated interaction, for many of them often appeared indifferent and uninterested, or perhaps annoyed, by human presence. But Obie was different. He walked right up to the rail and extended his big velvety nose to his friend, gently brushing his face.

"You are a gem, my friend," Earl said in a low tone, a smile on his face. He reached out and began to pet Obie's neck, rubbing behind the ears and working his way to the forehead, then gently touching his lips, which caused the horse to playfully bite at his fingertips. Some horses mistake fingers for carrots, and Earl made sure to pay close attention to the intensity of Obie's nibbling.

Earl had been a horse lover since birth. Even as a child who could barely walk, the big animals lured him in. Once his mother looked out the kitchen window while visiting relatives and was startled by the sight of the boy sitting among the small herd of horses beyond the fence. She gasped and turned to Richard, who was deep in a conversation until he saw the look of sheer terror on her face.

Richard sprang from his seat to the window. He looked out where she was pointing, and he made the mistake of grinning at the sight of his youngest son sitting in delight in the tall grass while the big animals walked and grazed all around him. Just then, one of the largest horses began to nuzzle his new little friend's head with his huge nose. Patricia's eyes grew large and fiery at the sight, and at that moment Richard lowered his head and walked briskly out the door in the direction of his son, still laughing quietly under his breath at the thought of the little squirt just sitting out there among the beasts. "That's my boy!" he said to himself, his heart all joy and pride.

Though he wouldn't normally endorse Earl being out there on his own, he figured there was no sense in crying over spilled milk and knew enough about these particular horses and their calm natures to not be too alarmed. Still, they were enormous and could easily be frightened, so he picked up his pace a little.

All these years later, Earl still couldn't stay away from the animals. He was lost in play with Obie when he heard the soft trot of another horse coming through the woods towards the barn.

Riding bareback on one of the seasoned geldings, eyes soft as the wind and strong as the oaks that bordered the sun-speckled trail that she emerged from, was Ruth. Earl swallowed hard, barely noticing Obie who was now nibbling softly at his ears.

"Earl," she said in a warm tone of surprise while leading the horse to the gate where Earl stood, her eyes looking briefly at his and then to the ground. "I wasn't expecting to see you out here."

"Well, I needed to get away from the crowd for a little while," he responded after a moment of formulating an answer, "and I heard a rumor that you might be out here." She blushed. "How was your ride?"

"Wonderful," she said softly. "I wish it never had to end. A few of us girls decided to go out together, and after returning I just couldn't help but go back out for a short ride by myself. It's just so beautiful out here, and this boy is so well-mannered. I'm sorry for missing you earlier."

"That's okay. My brother and I arrived late, and I'm glad you had the chance to get on the trails. You're riding one of the best ones out here."

Though Earl barely knew this girl, he could sense a change in her demeanor from the morning. It was almost as if being around the stables made her more wistful, more reflective. And the way she handled herself made it obvious that she was an experienced rider. She was confident, patient, and strong, gently caressing the animal many times while maintaining a firm yet tender authority. The animal was putty in her hands.

She soon dismounted and stood just feet from Earl as she removed the bridle.

"This is always one of my favorite parts," said Earl.

"Me too," she said softly. "It has to feel so liberating having this metal removed from the mouth."

"I would sure think so. For what it's worth, you'd be safe without a bridle with this one."

"I wondered about that. Not knowing him for more than an hour, though, I didn't want to take the chance."

"I understand," he responded. "One time I was riding with a few friends, one of whom thought the horse he had would obey without a bit. We encouraged him to use one since it was a retired barrel racer that was still relatively new here. He politely declined our advice. He'd ridden it for a few weeks and thought it would be just fine."

"And?" inquired Ruth, grinning with curiosity.

Earl laughed a little before answering, as he always did when retelling this story.

"Well, we set out on the trail, and for the first half hour all looked to be good. And then it happened."

"What happened?" asked Ruth, lightly laughing with anticipation.

"All of a sudden, with no warning whatsoever, the horse just decided to make a run for it. He took off galloping down the trail as fast as he could—and it wasn't slow by any means—with our friend hanging on for dear life. Soon they rounded a corner and disappeared from sight but not from sound. The galloping was like thunder.

"We weren't in any position to chase after him, though we did pursue, and up the trail a ways we saw his cowboy hat laying in the middle of the trail, but we still couldn't see them and could no longer hear them. So we rode on, and ten minutes later we saw them on the other side of the road, both of them huffing and puffing. Thankfully our friend was a good rider, otherwise it could have been ugly—likely would have been thrown into the woods when rounding some of the corners. He said he couldn't do anything to slow the horse down, and just held on tight as it sped on with no thought to turns in the trails or cars on the road they passed over."

"Oh my! And he was okay?"

"Yeah, he was fine, though a little shaken up and much more humble than before the ride. And very thankful to be alive."

Ruth laughed at his story, and they talked for a little while longer about the stables and all that came with them. Earl considered asking her if she'd like to ride together sometime, but something told him it was too soon to ask.

"I should be getting back to the picnic," said Ruth. "My parents are probably wondering if I lost my way on the trails."

"Good idea," replied Earl. "Can I walk this guy back to the pasture with you?"

"That would be wonderful, thank you," she said with a spring in her step as she gently took hold of the halter.

Earl climbed over the fence and came alongside her, and together they walked the horse through the gate and released it into the pasture. After a few steps the animal dropped to the ground with a thud and began rolling in the dirt as sounds of neighing came from all his friends. They looked on for a moment, enjoying the scene, before they turned around and began walking back to join the others.

Their return together did not go unnoticed, and more than a few people of this small town wondered if there was something brewing between these two young ones.

The rest of the afternoon passed quickly, and soon the picnic drew to a close. Those who remained began to say their goodbyes, and among the families remaining were the Timmings and the Bensons. Earl and Ruth stole a few glances at each other, eager as they were to speak to one another one last time before leaving.

Finally, just as the Timmings were about to leave, Ruth strolled over to Earl. "Thanks again for helping me," said Ruth, "and for sharing a good story with me."

"My pleasure," replied Earl. "I always seem to have a story or two lingering in my head, and I hope I didn't bore you with it."

"Definitely not," she responded, tilting her head slightly. "You told it well . . . and I'd like to hear more of your stories sometime."

"It's a deal," he said after a brief pause, encouraged by the invitation.

"Goodnight Earl," she finally said, turning to leave with her family.

"Goodnight Ruth."

The following Tuesday, Earl and his father ventured to the river after dinner to resume fly-fishing. Tom couldn't come due to a commitment with Ann, his girlfriend, and they did a fine job of harassing him for his decision.

After some talk of weather conditions and reports from other fishermen, Richard mentioned that he had a chance to meet and talk with Steven earlier that day. Earl's interest quickly shifted away from the water, listening attentively while continuing to work his line.

"He was impressed with you, son," said his father, who cast again before continuing, "and he appreciated in no small way the kindness and respect you showed his daughter."

"I cannot imagine a girl like her not being respected. She is so genuine." He paused for a moment before continuing. "And special."

Earl's words, and the way he spoke them, made his father light up inside. Though he knew better than to get overly excited at this point, he and Patricia had prayed often for their sons' future wives, and it was exciting to be confronted by the possibility that this could be the one for Earl.

"I was thinking of asking her to go for a ride this week," he continued.

"Sounds like a fine idea to me," said Richard as he finished his forward cast and watched as his fly gently landed on the water right behind an exposed rock.

"I also thought of asking her father for his approval. Part of me is concerned that he might find it too soon."

"You do what you feel is right, son," his father said, looking over at him. "I think he'd be okay with it, but you never know. Regardless, you can do no harm by going to him first." Richard sought to offer the best wisdom he could but was careful to leave the final call in his son's court.

"Thanks Dad," Earl said with appreciation and eagerness. "I'm going to do that."

The next morning, Earl rose from bed with a wave of eagerness that hit him even before his eyes fully opened. Today was the day that he was going to visit Mr. Benson during his lunch hour.

He knelt to pray and remained on his knees longer than normal. His anxious heart left him with much to say, and at one point he was reminded that more words equal less meaning, and that it is often better to be still and silent, and to listen. Yet he made his requests known, and did so with a childlike freedom. And one request stood at the top of this morning's list.

Afterward he took Danny for an extra-long walk, occasionally running through the trails and jumping over fallen logs or looking up into the skies or into the woods and feeling a friendly fire surge through his veins.

When they returned to the house, Earl showered and ate breakfast, then hopped in the truck with Danny and set out for work.

Earl was a talented carpenter who learned much of his skill from his father. He worked for a local home and cabin builder that was well known throughout the Northwoods, and his position often carried him and Danny from one town to another, sometimes for days at a time. While he truly enjoyed working with his hands, he also possessed an unyielding passion for literature and composition, which set him apart from his coworkers who often fed off his insights.

On this morning, Earl arrived to the shop in Mountain and began working on a project—building a custom oak desk for a local client—that he had begun a week earlier. Earl especially appreciated the task this morning, for it engaged his mind and body and distracted his thoughts that were consumed by Ruth. For obvious reasons, that morning passed more quickly into lunchtime than ever before, and he found himself anxiously walking up the steps of the building that would lead to Mr. Benson's office, his heart thumping inside once again.

"Hi ma'am, is Mr. Benson available?" he asked the receptionist.

"I believe he is. Let me see if he's in his office. May I ask your name?"

"Earl Timmings," he replied cordially.

"Oh, so you're one of the Timmings," she responded, her tone easing up a bit. "Pleased to meet you. I'm new to the area, but already I keep hearing good things about your family. One moment Earl. I'll see if he's here."

"Thank you," he gently replied.

The receptionist smiled and walked through a door and down a short hallway. He could hear bits and pieces of ensuing dialogue, though he was clearly able to hear the words: "Sure, send him in please." Earl's pulse quickened.

A moment later the receptionist reappeared with a smile. "Earl, Mr. Benson is available to meet with you," she said, then showed him through the door and pointed to his office.

Earl stopped at the door to the room and noticed Steven standing in front of a window. He was looking out over the street across the field, his arms crossed with one hand resting on his chin as if thinking intently. The field seemed unending. Earl knocked on the wood door, and Steven turned around methodically, pulling himself out of a moment of deep thought.

"Earl, good to see you. Come on in and have a seat," he said, while gesturing with his hand to the chair in front of the desk. "Can I get you something to drink? Perhaps a cup of coffee?"

"I'll have a small cup," Earl replied. He normally abstained from coffee beyond the morning hours, but not today.

"Great," responded Steven, who walked over to the coffeepot and poured two small cups.

"So, Earl, what brings you here today?" he asked while leaning against the front of his desk, though the topic of conversation was obvious.

Earl swallowed slightly and shifted forward a little in his seat, then composed himself and looked squarely into Steven's eyes. "I was hoping to ask your daughter to accompany me on a horseback ride this week, and I thought that since you and your family are still new in town and really don't know me that well, it would be best to ask for your blessing before doing so."

Steven smiled, sipped his coffee, then looked back at Earl winsomely and reached out his hand and gave Earl a firm handshake.

"Earl, thank you for your consideration. I'd be delighted if you took my daughter for a ride," he said warmly. "My one suggestion," he continued, walking back to the window to look outside before turning back to Earl, "don't waste any time in doing so. She is a special one."

Earl sat speechless for a moment, unsure how to respond to this most unexpected, encouraging response.

"Uh, thank you, Mr. Benson," Earl responded, relieved and thrilled, clearing his throat before continuing. "I will heed your advice."

After talking for a short time, Steven indicated that it was time to return to work. Earl thanked him for his time, then excused himself.

"Oh, one more thing Earl," said Steven as Earl was about to pass through the door. Earl stopped and turned, half expecting to receive some sort of qualification. "She will be home tonight around six, if that helps any."

"That does," Earl replied with a grin, grateful for the budding alliance. "Thank you again, sir."

Earl returned to work that afternoon with an extra bounce in his step, and though he kept the source of his heightened state confidential, his coworkers had a good hunch. The day passed quickly, and afterward Earl drove home to eat and shower.

"Earl, what's the occasion?" his mother asked lightheartedly as he was putting his shoes on. He was not normally one to shower after work unless really dirty, and it tipped her off that something was out of the ordinary.

"I have an invitation to give to someone," he said grinning, knowing that his mother would be craving more details. At this, her head turned slightly to the side and her eyes narrowed into that investigative look that her family knew so well. She then looked to Richard who was sitting at the kitchen table reading the newspaper. He grinned, knowing that his wife now had him under surveillance.

"You guys are not telling me something here," said Patricia, causing them both to laugh.

"Dad can fill you in. I gotta run," he replied as he strode for the door. "C'mon Danny!"

Earl drove a touch faster than normal, and was relieved to find Ruth home, just as her father had indicated. Earl walked up the steps to the screen door and knocked gently. It looked as if they had just finished dinner, for he could hear the sounds of water running, dishes clinking, and light conversation.

A moment later, Ruth came to the door. Earl could feel a lump in his throat.

"Earl, what a surprise to see you here!" she said with a sweet smile that helped ease his tension.

"Hi Ruth," he responded. "I hope I didn't interrupt your dinner."

"Not at all! We're just cleaning up before going into town for some shopping."

"Good," he replied. He was a little short on breath, and Ruth's heart beat a little faster when she perceived this. "I won't keep you long," he continued. "I just came by to see if you'd like to join me on a horseback ride this week," he said, swallowing hard after forcing the words out. "There are all kinds of great trails around here that I think you'd enjoy."

Ruth tilted her head to the side, then smiled warmly as her eyes grew with excitement.

"Yes! I would love to."

Earl had often wondered what it would feel like to be struck by lightning, and now he knew that he had a small taste.

"Great!" he responded, doing his best to keep his satisfaction from oozing out of him. "Would this Saturday morning work? I could pick you up, and we could drive to the stables together."

"Perfect," she responded. Then they both stood there quietly looking at each other, motionless other than Ruth gently petting Danny's head that was now leaning heavily into her thigh. Suddenly, Danny moaned in delight loud enough to evoke their laughter, breaking the comfortable silence. Ruth's mother then came to the door, not wanting Earl to leave without first greeting him.

After a few minutes of conversation, Earl excused himself so that they could finish cleaning up and go shopping, and he and Danny climbed back into the truck. He gave one final wave to Ruth and her mother, who remained on the porch talking and watching the truck depart.

"Good work, Danny!" Earl said as they motored down the driveway and onto the road. "You may have just helped me land the best horseback ride ever."

As the cool wind blew through the truck, Earl felt finer than he could ever recall. Danny looked over at him with his big eyes, his tail thumping away, then returned to the passenger window and stuck his head out as far as possible to catch the wind.

"Enjoy that wind, friend," said Earl, contented over Danny's enjoyment and knowing exactly how he felt. Earl then turned to look out his own window, believing that Saturday could not possibly come soon enough.

Spring Awakening

May 30, 1942—Saturday evening
From Earl's journal

I could have ridden across the country with that girl today. She is one of the most enjoyable people I have ever been around. And while there are many moments that would deserve a place in this journal, I especially recall looking back once when I was in the lead, seeing her gazing off into the woods with a look of pure contentment on her face, then down to her horse and up at me. I felt like I was caught, and surprisingly, I didn't care. She is beautiful.

Saturday morning came quickly. Earl continued with his morning routine by brewing coffee and walking outside with Danny to admire the starry morning sky, then sat down to read a chapter of Proverbs and capture thoughts and reflections in his journal. He and Ruth had talked about getting on the trails at daybreak, and he was determined to prevent even one minute from slipping away.

Earl picked up Ruth and together they drove out to the Harmons' stables, where they had just been a week earlier for the picnic. Earl discovered that Ruth had a horse of her own that she kept in the barn by her house, but since he was still growing accustomed to the new surroundings, they felt it would be best for her to ride one of the regulars.

They eagerly saddled the horses and set out down the tree-lined path that led into the forest and to a host of trails. Earl rode Obie and Ruth rode Moses, the same horse she rode during the picnic. Moses was a middle-aged gelding that possessed an incredibly gentle, loving, and obedient demeanor, and was one of the favorites for all who visited these stables. Earl led, though they changed positions more than once.

In no hurry whatsoever, they talked about books they both enjoyed, before moving on to different breeds of horses and dogs and the different temperaments they possessed. They shared stories about growing up and places they had visited. Earl told her about his house and some of the plans he had for it, and Ruth shared her aspirations of becoming a nurse. All the while, both were filled with energy and the sense of not wanting to be anywhere else, thoroughly enjoying each other's company. And mixed in were moments of silence, in which both were mesmerized by the rays of sunlight that continued to shoot through the forest, illuminating remnants of the morning mist that still hung softly in the air. The air itself was so fresh and moist, and more than once, both riders noticed the other breathing it in deeply.

"Earl, I know little of northern Wisconsin, though so far you've given me a great taste of it. This land is magical."

"I'm glad you feel that way," replied Earl. "Sometimes I take it for granted, but it's difficult to on mornings like this."

"I understand," she replied softly. "We used to go riding on a nearby forest preserve outside of town near our old home in Iowa. It was breathtaking as well, so peaceful. And as I look back, I wish I would've taken advantage of it more often." Earl watched her expression as she spoke, and could sense a touch of disappointment in her tone.

"I'm sorry," he responded. "Unfortunately, I don't think we've got time to ride to Iowa, and well, I don't know if Moses would make it that far anyway, but perhaps we can help each other take advantage of these trails."

"That's a deal!" said Ruth cheerfully, lifting her stare from the ground in front of her and back at Earl, who now rode behind her.

After ascending a hill and then descending down and around a corner, they came to a place along the trail that was close to the lake, with a small clearing that provided easy access.

"Let's stop here for a minute and let the horses have a quick drink," said Earl.

They dismounted and unbridled the horses, then walked them to the water. Earl and Ruth sat on the grass just a few yards away, both facing the calm waters while leaning back, their hands on the ground behind them acting as support.

Earl felt a bit nervous while sitting there next to Ruth, more so than he expected. And in his mind Ruth seemed perfectly poised, though in reality she was nervous too. While talking, Earl pointed out an eagle flying in the distance, and accidently touched her hand when bringing his back to the ground.

"I'm sorry," he said, his face turning a light shade of red.

"That's okay," responded Ruth, blushing herself.

A short time passed before they were back in their saddles and on the trail, and not long after they came to a section that was straight and even, well suited for higher speeds. Earl knew the trail well, and prompted Obie to pick up the pace by gently squeezing with his legs and making a clucking noise. While they refrained from an all-out gallop, they cantered at a good clip for several minutes. At one point, Earl briefly glanced back at Ruth and could see a wide, exhilarated expression on her face that heightened his adrenaline.

"That was amazing!" exclaimed Ruth as they began to slow down.

Earl just looked at her and grinned.

They rode on for another ten minutes and eventually came to the trail that led back to the stables, and both riders could feel the anticipation in their horses. Some things never change; among those is a horse's desire to return home. And they knew exactly when they were doing so.

On the contrary, neither Earl nor Ruth wanted the ride to end, but both sensed that this was only the first of many rides.

Soon they were back in Earl's truck and on the road to Ruth's, conversation rolling the entire way there. When they pulled up, Earl walked her to her door and thanked her for joining him.

"Earl, thank *you*. That was a wonderful ride."

"My pleasure," he responded. "And you're a great rider." Ruth silently beamed at his words.

"Well," said Earl during a pause in their conversation. "I suppose I'd better be going." He nodded, then excused himself and walked away. He wanted to ask her out again immediately, though was concerned that he may be rushing her, so he held back once again.

"Goodbye, Earl. Thank you again," she said longingly. Earl looked back at her and held her gaze before continuing on his way. Ruth lingered on the porch for a moment, wanting him to stay, then went inside and closed the screen door behind her, watching his truck pull away.

Inside, her parents were sitting at the table, concealing their heightened curiosity as best they could.

"How was the ride, honey?"

"Wonderful," she said with a sigh.

"Is he still here?"

"No," she said in a soft voice, "he's just driving away now." Her parents looked at each other, grinning over the deeper meaning that they detected in her voice.

"Why don't you ask him to dinner here tonight?" her mother suggested.

Ruth's eyes brightened, and in a moment the screen door was flung open and she was running down the gravel driveway towards the departing truck.

"Tell him to bring his dog too!" her father shouted.

To her delight, she saw the truck slow and come to a stop. Collecting herself just a little, she approached the driver's side window.

"Earl, would you like to join us for dinner tonight? Around six o'clock?"

"Yes," Earl responded without hesitation, pleased by the surprise invitation. "I would definitely like that."

"Good!" she said smiling, still catching her breath. "Then we'll see you tonight."

"Great," Earl affirmed.

Ruth started walking towards the house but spun around. "Oh! I almost forgot. Danny's presence was requested as well."

Earl laughed and nodded in acknowledgment. Then he waved, put the truck into first, and continued on down the driveway while keeping one eye on his rearview mirror.

"Lookin' sharp, son," said Richard, who was sitting at the kitchen table fiddling with his fly rod and reel when Earl emerged from his bedroom.

"Yeah, looks like you're going to see a girl or something," said Tom, a grin on his face as he reached for a bowl of peanuts on the table and shoveled a handful into his mouth. He sat opposite his father at the table, preparing his own rod.

"Thanks Dad, and good observation Tom," responded Earl, who was clean shaven and well-dressed in a nice flannel, new pair of jeans, and polished boots.

"Looking sharp indeed," said Patricia, who went to the fridge and pulled out a small package. "Take this with you tonight. There are a couple jars of homemade raspberry jam and some brownies for Ruth and her family."

"Thanks Mom, though I may just eat these on the way," he said while taking the package from her.

"You do that, and I'll tell Ruth at church tomorrow," she said, raising on eyebrow in victory. Stephanie, who sat at the table across from Richard and Tom drawing a picture, giggled.

"You win," he conceded. "All right, all, I have to leave now. Are we still on for fishing tomorrow afternoon?" he said, looking at the guys at the table, their faces deep in concentration.

"Absolutely!" replied Richard and Tom simultaneously. Earl grinned, then eagerly made his way out of the house.

Earl turned the ignition key and set out. Eager to reach his destination, he drove a little faster than usual, and it seemed like just as soon as he pulled out of the drive he was already walking up to Ruth's door and then in the company of her and her family.

"Ruth, dinner is almost ready and I can finish the rest. Why don't you take Earl out back and enjoy some fresh air by the water?" Cynthia noticed Earl admiring the view of their land through the glass door in the dining room.

"I second that suggestion. I can help your mother if she needs it," added Steven, winking at his wife in a playful spirit. He was a talented man in many ways, but his usefulness in the kitchen had much to be desired—except for when it came to fish and venison, and that he could only prepare outside over a fire.

"Oh, all right, then. Just don't eat those brownies Dad," laughed Ruth as they walked out the back door.

"Don't worry; I'll leave one for you and Earl to share."

Ruth led Earl outside, and they walked towards the oval-shaped pond that sat just fifty yards from the house. There was a small bench on the bank that faced west and provided a pleasant view of the calm waters. Ruth stopped near this bench for a moment and began pointing out details of the landscape before continuing to walk the perimeter of the pond. Farmland and vast, spring-green fields stretched far and wide to the north and were bordered by a dense forest. To the west, a hundred yards away on the other side of the country road that ran northwest along the southern border of their property, sat an old, rustic barn that was enclosed by a wood rail fence with tall grass and numerous large boulders surrounding it, along with two horses leisurely grazing. The barn seemed ageless, appearing to be in good condition, and Earl could not help but take several looks at it.

Soon Earl and Ruth heard her mother's voice calling them to dinner and returned to the house. Earl was a little nervous at first, but he soon settled in and found himself at ease with this family, who clearly enjoyed hosting and easily made their guests feel welcomed. Within minutes, he felt strangely at home.

After dinner, Earl and Steven went and sat out on the back porch for a few minutes before being joined by the others. They all decided to go for a walk together down the road, and set out immediately before the night swallowed up the light. Along the way they stopped at the barn so that Ruth could show Earl her horse, which she had been eager to do all night.

"Here's my boy!" Ruth said proudly. "His name is Samuel. Pure quarter horse." The chestnut gelding neighed and began walking towards her, then extended his neck over the fence and gently nuzzled her face.

"He's a good-looking horse," said Earl. "And he sure adores you."

Soon they continued walking, the fresh air on their faces and the clear sky above them, Steven and Danny pulling each other around while playing tug of war with a stick.

Upon return, Ruth's parents went inside and left Earl and Ruth to themselves out back. Drawn by the setting sun, they walked side by side to the bench and sat down.

"Sure is peaceful out here," said Earl, in a calm voice that underscored his words. He felt sedated by the combination of the view and his full stomach.

"I know. I love coming out here to just sit and take it all in. And the beauty around here has helped ease the settling in process." Earl hung on her words, which were spoken with gentle passion as she sat upright, slightly angled towards him and fully engaged.

"I can imagine," he replied. "There is something powerful about water and long stretching fields that draws a person in." He paused for a moment, and then looked to his left. "There is something about that barn too."

"I agree," she said with fondness in her voice. "I hope it never goes away. It sits so still and nostalgic, like something you'd expect to see in a painting."

Shortly before the Bensons had moved into the house, they were considering building a small stable for their horses. They were about to hire a builder when they were contacted by the owner of the barn who offered to sell it to them. He no longer farmed, he said, and wanted to see the land go to us. He was a kind, older man whose wife's health was in decline, and the price he communicated was far below what Steven would have been willing to pay. Steven even offered to pay him more, convinced it was worth it, but the old man would have nothing to do with any price other than the one he offered.

> "*Mr. Benson*, I'll give it to you for this price, and that's final," he said, sternness and healthy pride in

his deep voice. "You and your family come to this town with a reputation of bein' honest and generous, and therefore I have no room for negotiations on the matter."

"Yes sir," replied Steven. "In that case, we'd be honored to buy it. But only if you agree to come over for dinner after we get settled in."

"That I can agree too, sir. That I can definitely agree to. I hope the land and barn is a blessin' to you all. It has been to us."

"I believe it will be. We can't thank you enough."

"Don't need to. Just feed me," said the man with a big smile that sealed the agreement.

"What is your place like?" said Ruth, gently shifting the conversation away from the barn.

"It's picturesque too, though in a different way. Our house sits on a small clearing surrounded by a forest full of hardwoods and big pines. Behind the house is a trail that meanders down to a small lake that Danny and I often go down to. There is a little bench down there too, sort of like this one, and a canoe."

"That sounds wonderful," she said gently.

"I could show you sometime, if you like."

"I'd like that," she said after a moment with a hint of eagerness in her voice, looking briefly at Earl then back to the water and sky.

"Well, how about this Friday? You could join my family and me for dinner."

"Let me check with my parents first to see if we have obligations that night. If not, I would love to."

"Good," he responded, secretly admiring the way the sun was casting a golden glow upon her face. Not wanting to be caught staring, he looked away from her and to the water and sunset, which was now at its peak, touching every living thing for miles around with a fingertip of breathtaking beauty and serenity.

It wasn't until the passing of twilight that the two returned to the house, where they ate Patricia's brownies and played a board game with her parents until everyone began to tire. No one really wanted the evening to end, but they kept noticing each other yawning and knew the inevitable was coming.

"Thank you for joining us tonight, Earl. It was a delight having you here," said Cynthia. "And please thank your mother for the brownies and jam. They are delicious."

"I second that," responded Steven with a tired, contented voice.

"I'll be sure to let her know. Thank you again for the dinner and hospitality," said Earl before he walked out the door, Ruth escorting him out.

"I really enjoyed the time with you and your family," he said as they slowly walked side by side to his truck.

"Not as much as we enjoyed having you," she said as Earl placed his hand on the door handle. "I'll—oh, wait one minute!" She turned and went quickly into the house, then returned a moment later having secured permission. "I'll see you Friday, at your house."

"Great! We'll be ready for you," he responded.

"Goodnight, Earl," she said softly, then slowly walked away and remained on the porch, where she stood and watched him drive off until his lights were out of sight.

June 5, 1942
From Earl's journal

    I am young, and the miles under my feet are few, though I believe tonight was one of those experiences that will never leave me.

> At one point this evening I wished that I was Danny, only to be so close to Ruth as we drove to her house. Yet I know there is a time for things, and I'm grateful and honored that I was able to be with her at all.

The next week, Earl was sitting anxiously on the front porch waiting for Ruth to arrive when he heard the sound of lightly crunching gravel coming from down the driveway, hidden by the forest. Danny, lounging next to him, shot up and began trotting in the direction of the noise, barking with a deep, authoritative tone, his tail high and wagging with a mixture of excitement and apprehension. Soon, Ruth's face came into view, riding on her bike with a look of pure contentment on her face. Her face lit up at the sight of Danny, who bolted the rest of the way to meet her, his tail wagging furiously.

"Oh, Danny!" she said, hopping off her bike to bend over to pet and hug him. "So good to see you sweetie!" Danny's eyes grew heavy, and he moaned with delight.

Earl lit up when he saw her, both impressed and surprised at her choice of transportation.

"You rode your bicycle the entire way?"

"I did, and it was wonderful," she said with a passion in her voice that Earl found contagious. "And the weather was perfect for it." She rode up a little further and stepped off her bike, then looked at him with spirited eyes. "How are you?"

"It's been a good day," he said with a beaming smile that he didn't care to hide, "and I'm glad you made it here. Can I take your vehicle for you?"

"Yes, thank you," she said warmly. Earl took the bike, then carefully walked it over to the porch steps and leaned it against the wood railing.

"I bet this thing is great on gas," he said after positioning it carefully.

"Extremely!" she laughed.

After lingering outside for a few minutes, they walked inside where Ruth was greeted by the rest of the family. She was impressed by how warm and welcoming they were—like her own family, she thought—treating her as if she were a special, honored guest.

They soon took their seats at the table and enjoyed a pleasant meal with lively conversation as the sun shone through the windows. Everyone was delighted by Ruth's company, especially little Stephanie who sat next to her. Tom's girlfriend, Ann, was there too, and her kind, outgoing personality contributed to Ruth's comfort. Though this wasn't the first time Richard and Patricia had met Ruth, they were newly impressed by her. They could easily see why Earl was drawn to this girl from Iowa. In a way that was rare for someone her age, she carried herself well and was comfortable in her own skin. There was something about her that made others feel at ease. She chose her words carefully and was also a great listener. But Richard and Patrica's favorite quality was her rich, life-giving laugh.

"Earl is done for," whispered Richard close into Patricia's ear while getting up for more coffee. "Just like I was with you." Patricia blushed and failed to conceal her grin. Conversation rolled on around the table, though no one, including Tom—who was usually caught up in energized banter, missed this loving, secretive exchange.

"What did he say?" asked Stephanie innocently.

"Oh, sweetie," she responded lovingly, "just that he really enjoyed the meal."

"Sure he did," said Tom, who was lightly kicked under the table by Ann.

After the meal, Ruth offered to help Patricia clean up. But she had not expected to see the guys take the lead in this—her father was one of the few men she had ever seen help clean up after a meal.

After cleaning up and enjoying dessert and coffee at the table, Earl escorted Ruth out the back door and gave her a tour of the yard. They walked the perimeter of the house, then made for the trail that led to the lake, which Ruth so eagerly wanted to see.

With Danny out in front and all around, the two walked down the descending, tree-lined trail. From every step the lake could be seen in the distance, and on this clear night, the sun's rays were shining brightly on the waters, luring the trio down the path.

"This is beautiful," said Ruth whimsically as they arrived to the clearing at the water's edge.

"We have lived here for a long time, and I still think those same words to myself every time I come down here," replied Earl, enjoying the privilege of being able to share this special place with her.

Ruth walked straight to the bench and sat down, stately yet relaxed, and took a deep breath. There was a mixture of peace and exhilaration on her face as she looked out over the expanse of the calm waters. Earl, perceiving her enjoyment, slowly sat down next to her and looked out over the water.

"You must come down here a lot," she said softly after a few moments, looking over at him.

"I do," he replied, feeling her eyes on him, the power of her gaze. "I often come down here in the morning to start the day. Other times, especially after work, I come down and just sit, quiet and alone, to unwind and reflect on life."

"I think I'd do the same thing," replied Ruth, her eyes fixed ahead. She then slowly repositioned herself in her seat, turning ever so slightly towards him, and then continued, "What's one of your favorite books, or pieces of literature?"

"Ecclesiastes," he said immediately. She was both surprised and impressed by his decisive answer. "I appreciate how it reminds us of the brevity of life, and that our days are numbered and are to be enjoyed fully within the parameters of God. There are many other truths in it too that have a way of speaking to me at random times in my life; many that I trust will speak even more loudly as I get some more years under my belt."

Ruth hung on to his words while contemplating how few guys there were his age who reflected on deep things like this.

"I like that too. One of my favorites is the part where it speaks of eternity being placed in our hearts, and that everything is beautiful in its time . . ." she paused, searching for the right words, "like . . . what we're looking at right now."

Earl thought how the moment itself was beautiful in its time—the two of them sitting there with no interruption before the calm waters and radiant skies.

"That canoe over there," she said, breaking the momentary silence that neither of them knew they were in the midst of. "Is that yours?"

"It sure is," he said with a proud voice. "We've put a lot of miles on that thing."

"Danny goes with you too?"

"Always, though admittedly he sometimes gets a little nervous while in it. Thankfully his desire to be at my side exceeds his anxiety over open waters."

Ruth laughed and looked down at Danny, who came close when hearing his name and looked endearingly into Earl's eyes.

"He simply adores you," she said. "You must treat him well."

"I'd like to think so. He is such a good boy," replied Earl, rubbing Danny's his ears.

"He sure is. If you ever need someone to watch him while you're away, please come to me first," she said while reaching down and doing the same. Once Danny felt her touch, he leaned his head over and placed it on her lap and looked her in the eyes. She melted immediately.

"I see he's got you captive," he said smiling. "Just so you know, he doesn't let go."

"Good. I don't want him to," replied Ruth in a soft tone. Then she sniffled lightly before looking away.

"Are you okay?" he asked after a moment.

"Oh, yes," she said. "It's just that your dog reminds me of our last dog, who passed away shortly before we moved here." Earl noticed her eyes growing moist. "He was fifteen years old and had been a part of our family for as long as I remember. Healthy and active right up until the last few months of his life."

"I'm sorry," said Earl. "That had to be so hard on all of you."

"It was, and we all miss him so much. We hoped he could be a part of our new life here, but it was his time." At this, her voice broke. "But he lived a good long life," she continued, recomposing herself, "and for that we're grateful. And you bringing Danny over to our house was good for us all."

Earl looked her in the eyes for a few moments, allowing the brief silence to linger, then looked over in the direction of the canoe.

"Would you like to go for a ride around the lake?" he asked, sensing that she needed respite from the conversation.

"I would love to," she replied while wiping away a tear.

Together they walked to the canoe, eager but unhurried. Earl wiped off the seats with an old towel that he took from the small boathouse and then invited Ruth to enter, holding it steady for her as she stepped in. She boarded with ease, showing that this was not the first time in a canoe.

With a little bit of encouragement, Danny jumped in after her. As usual, he was a bit wary, though Ruth did her best to comfort him.

"I'm sure he appreciates your compassion out here," Earl said with a grin. "He usually does not receive it from me when we're on the water."

"How come?"

"I feel like it's my responsibility to toughen him up a bit, put him in some challenging situations to help him overcome his fear."

"Are you being serious?" asked Ruth, wearing a slight grin herself, while wondering if she was beginning to unearth Earl's dry sense of humor. He avoided looking her in the eye when saying it, which added to her curiosity.

"Half-serious, depending on the day of the week," he responded while taking the first major stroke with the paddle and propelling them away from the shore.

"I see," she said laughing. "I'd like to contribute to his inner growth as well, though I may act as more of an encourager."

"Perfect. You can provide the missing balance," he said smiling. "In all seriousness, once we're out here for a while, he starts to ease up a bit when he notices all the little critters running around on the shore and the fish and bugs moving in the water."

Their conversation continued to flow with increasing comfort, talking of both light and deeper matters—family, faith, work, pets, literature, and a host of other topics. There were also times of brief silence. But neither found these moments uncomfortable. A few times Earl felt compelled to make conversation, though he did his best to hold back and simply enjoy it. He had learned that men are more prone to try to fix things that aren't always broken, and in this case, nothing was in need of repair. But of course there were a few moments where he just couldn't hold back. Thankfully, Ruth graciously overlooked this, and instead saw a young man who was trying, and she was delighted by his effort.

And so they went, both admiring the blue sky and the way the stars began to appear one by one, the quarter-moon that gradually rose in the horizon. Danny provided for a bit of laughter too. On a couple of occasions, he saw something in the water that caused him to lean as far over the side as he could, placing one paw on the edge to steady himself, and with the other paw he would reach out for it, just tapping the surface of the water.

"What is it buddy?" Earl whispered loudly, trying to rouse his friend's spirit. Danny would look over at him with wide, wild eyes, seemingly yearning for his master to help him get whatever was down there. Then he'd return his attention to the water, growling and whining simultaneously.

Earl rowed on slowly, pointing out different spots on the lake and the history behind them. The air was beginning to grow considerably cooler, and he offered his flannel to Ruth, who accepted it without reservation. She was getting a little cold, though this was trumped by the simple allure of wearing his flannel.

"What is something you fear, Earl?" she asked softly after a few moments of silence, turning slightly in her seat to face him. Earl paused for a moment, pleasantly caught off guard by the question. "Sorry, I tend to spring deep questions on people when they're not expecting it."

"That's okay," he responded. "I like that." He made another stroke with the paddle, the sounds of water trickling down the oar and back into the water now more noticeable, his eyes revealing the turning wheels in his mind. "Something I fear . . ." He went silent for a moment, then stopped paddling. "Dying while I'm still breathing."

Ruth sat motionless for a moment, then turned to look towards the shoreline, obviously in deep thought. She then turned back to him with a look that said *"Tell me more."*

"I've known people who, for whatever reasons, seem to be just floating along in life, not really going anywhere nor wanting to. Some who seem like walking tombs, lacking any sort of passion and purpose." He paused and took a large stroke with the paddle. "My dad helped me understand that many of these people have been dealt some heavy blows from life—many that I have not yet experienced and may never." He paused, taking another stroke with the paddle. "But I never want to end up like that." He looked forward at Ruth, who just sat listening attentively, affirming his words with her intentional silence and fixed stare.

"Thank you for sharing that," she responded gently after a few moments. "I believe I know some people like that too. Thankfully, the candle never completely goes out."

"Thankfully," he responded in agreement. "What about you? What is something you fear?"

"I guess similar to yours in a way." She paused and looked out over the water. "I fear being caged up, unable to run. I don't necessarily mean physically, but rather freedom to reach out and make a difference, to drink from life. I enjoy the kitchen, but I don't want to be confined to one."

Earl paddled gently and pondered her words.

"Though I barely know you, I don't see you ever being bound or confined to a kitchen."

Ruth took in a deep breath and exhaled, then returned a soft smile. She realized that she had never felt more comfortable opening up to a guy than she did now, remarkable since she had only known him for so brief a time. *"Enjoy this, Ruth, but keep watch over your heart. There is a time for things,"* she said to herself.

Little did she know that Earl was telling himself the same thing.

As twilight began to fade, they conceded that it was time to go back to the cabin. Earl rowed into shore and stepped barefoot out into the shallow water, pulling the canoe further up onto land. Danny jumped out and waited for Ruth, then bounded up the trail in front of them. The two walked leisurely, Ruth moving close to Earl's side as they were engulfed by the darkness caused by the canopy of trees above.

Upon arriving to the top of the hill, they were greeted by the glow of a campfire burning in the backyard and the family sitting contently around it.

"We saved a couple seats for you two," said Richard.

"Oh, this feels good," said Ruth, standing close to the fire before taking a seat, the heat quickly penetrating her chilled body.

It felt so good to be sitting around the fire, and it was obvious to all that these two enjoyed one another's company. Earl's parents noticed the content demeanor in their son and were so pleased to see it. Like any young man, he could be a bit hardheaded and impetuous at times, though it seemed as if Ruth's presence touched him with a cool ember that caused these traits to melt away. And they couldn't help but catch the looks that the two of them exchanged as the firelight danced on their faces.

"The way of a man with a maiden," Richard whispered into Patricia's ear at one point. Patricia sighed, thinking back to the days of courtship with her husband. Again, the rest of the family wondered about the exchange, but no one said anything. They simply smiled, enjoying their presence.

After a while of sitting and talking before the flames and enjoying coffee, hot chocolate and campfire treats, Tom went inside and returned with his guitar. Ann's face lit up at the sight of it. Tom was a gifted singer and songwriter, and he had a way of lulling his listeners into a trance with his smooth rhythm and steady, powerful voice.

Tom had played in front of the church on occasion, as well as other local venues. Occasionally, he and Ann would pack up the car and travel to towns near and far for small concerts, and they always return thrilled at the experience regardless of the size of the audience.

"You never know, little sis, though fame is not worth seeking," he once said when Stephanie asked him if he would someday be a famous musician and travel the world. "I just enjoy doing this, and pray that it will touch others."

His favorite place to play, though, was around the campfire, where the elements often worked together to bring everyone a little closer to heaven's shores. And on this particular night, he again took his listeners there. For almost an hour he played on, sometimes singing solo, sometimes just strumming, and as often as he could, ushering the others to sing along and send soft, beautiful voices up from the fire in harmony, riding on the backs of the sparks and filling the forest and skies all around them.

Eventually, as the flames simmered down and the guitar was laid at Tom's feet, the desire for bed brought the evening to a close.

"Thank you so much for having me here tonight," said Ruth as she stood with Richard and Patricia by the door. "You have such a wonderful family."

"It was our pleasure, Ruth. We hope to have you join us again. After all, campfire season is now in full swing," said Patricia, and then she gave Ruth a hug goodbye.

"I'll put your bike in the truck," said Earl. Ruth smiled warmly, recalling his offer in the canoe to give her a ride home so she could stay later—which was just what she had hoped for.

Down the gravel drive they went, both considerably tired but still not ready to let the night end. Danny was sitting between the two, resting his head on Ruth's lap.

"My dad would be grateful for Danny right now," she said with a smirk.

"How come?" Earl asked, looking over briefly as the truck moved slowly onto the road from the driveway.

"For sitting between us while we're alone," she responded with a smile, looking over at Earl with playful eyes.

Earl grinned as his eyes returned to the road, attracted to her wit and spontaneity that was coupled with a strong air of integrity. His interactions with her had made it clear to Earl that this young woman was saving herself for one person, and that by the grace of God she had the strength and support to do so.

"Yes, Danny is a true gentleman, always looking out for others," said Earl while briefly looking at the dog, who was now sprawled out over Ruth's lap as if drugged. "And if you haven't noticed, he tends to shut down around this time."

Seemingly aware that he was the center of attention, Danny briefly lifted his head and looked at both of them with half-opened eyes as Ruth rubbed his ears, then put his head down again. "Are you sure you're okay with him snuggling with you like that? I don't want him to get in trouble with your father . . ."

Ruth leaned her head back and laughed warmly. "I think Dad would be okay with this guy."

Down the road they went, Earl purposefully driving slower than usual. Ruth noticed the slow speed but said nothing, desiring the evening to linger on as far as possible.

All too soon, though, the lights of the Benson house came into view as they drove through the clearing of trees. After pulling to a stop, Earl stepped out and opened the door for Ruth.

"Thank you, Earl," she said as she stepped down from the truck. "I had a wonderful time tonight."

"Me too; I'm glad you were able to come." He paused for a moment, then continued, "I'll call you tomorrow?"

"I'd like that," she replied softly. "Goodnight, Earl."

"Goodnight, Ruth," he responded.

Earl watched her turn and walk to the door, then climbed back into the truck. Looking back once, he could see her looking at him from the door, and he kept his eye on her until out of view.

Though for the entire drive home and while lying in bed that night, he could still clearly see her standing there.

"I think it's time to put the shotgun away," said Steven into his wife's ear as they curled up into bed that night.

"I think so," said Cynthia with a tired laugh, squeezing his arm simultaneously. "I don't believe this young man is going to give you any reason to use it."

Steven sighed. "I always hoped for at least one opportunity to shoot at a fella's truck. Just once . . ."

"Sorry, love," she said, her laughter growing louder this time, "but you may have to let this one go."

In the bathroom, Ruth could faintly hear her parents' laughter while brushing her teeth.

June 5, 1942—Bedtime reflections after a night at the Timmings
From Ruth's journal

I could hear my parents' laughter while brushing my teeth tonight, and it warmed my heart beyond words. I cannot deny the longing within me to one day share such laughter and joy with another, and tonight, my heart aches with it.

Nor can I deny that there is one who now inspires laughter and joy within me, and does so in a way that is more pleasurable than any I have ever experienced. He is kind, sweet, genuine, and handsome, and when I'm with him, I want to be nowhere else. Yet I've known him for such a short time, and I pray for patience and the strength to keep my heart from running away, at least too fast, as we get to know each other.

I do not know which part of this evening was the most enjoyable. Was it the anticipation-filled ride to his house through another beautiful spring day, with air that tasted so sweet, and all the beauty of the countryside calling out to me as I rode on? The freedom I felt was overwhelming, and in some strange way, the sounds of gravel crunching underneath the tires and the wide-open skies fed my desire for adventure.

Or was it passing through Mountain and seeing the people and families go about life? I know that only God can truly read hearts, though I saw people who appeared to be so weary and burdened, and I could almost feel the grief and loneliness hidden behind their masked faces. I could also feel the joy of families, especially children, who laughed together while bounding out of small stores and trotting down the street.

Soon the town was behind me, and I was again in the countryside. I passed by farms and long driveways that led to houses where people were cutting firewood and doing other chores, young children jumping in spring puddles with reckless abandon, and elderly folk sitting contently outside on benches wearing slightly more clothing than others to keep warm. I do wonder what they think about, with all the years and memories they have accumulated, all the hellos and goodbyes.

As I rode on, an enormous flock of geese flying north passed over me, returning from their winter vacation in warm, southern climates. I could hear them coming long before they came into view. I even saw a mother and two fawns pass by on the road, at which point I stopped and just watched them. They are so beautiful and serene.

Maybe, though, just maybe, it was the first sight of Earl and Danny as I rode up their long gravel driveway. My heart raced when seeing him standing there, strong and humble, with that handsome crooked smile inviting me in.

It may have been the canoe ride on the lake, and our conversation in which Earl become more expressive, his introversion giving way to both deep thoughts and simple musings. Soon twilight began to descend upon us, bringing a surreal feeling that caused our words to grow fewer and our comfort to increase. The sounds of crickets and far off animals, some seemingly not as far-off as I would have preferred, began to grow in volume.

Or could it have been the time sitting around the campfire next to Earl and his family, wearing his flannel shirt that he gave me to keep warm during the canoe ride. Every muscle in my body was relaxed, my smile perpetual, the heat of the flame, the sweetness of the fellowship, and the sounds of Tom's guitar making time, the ticking of a clock, seem nonexistent and otherworldly.

Finally, it may have been the ride home in Earl's truck, where I could have fallen asleep with Danny on my lap, so content.

I'm going to concede that I cannot pick one, but rather take it all as one wonderful evening, and hope for more times with him in the future.

Thank you God, regardless of where things go. You know my desires.

Summer Bliss and Falling Leaves

"Hi, Mrs. Benson. This is Earl," he said, holding the phone up to his ear the next morning as he anxiously looked out the kitchen window. He had been alternately sitting and pacing for ten minutes before picking up the phone, wondering if he was rushing things by calling so soon. Finally, courage won out. "Is Ruth available?"

"Well good morning, Earl! It's good to hear from you," she said in a reassuring voice. "Ruth is here. Let me get her for you."

Earl could hear her mother set the phone down and call out to her daughter, who came to the phone seconds later.

"Hello?" Her voice was so full of life and zest that it caused Earl to sit up straighter in his seat.

"Hi Ruth," he said gently, trying to keep his voice steady. "This is—"

"Earl," she broke in warmly, "I was hoping it would be you."

"I realize this is short notice," he continued, "but I'm going to go out on the trails this evening, and was wondering if you'd like to ride with me."

"I would love to."

After saying goodbye, Earl hung up the phone and took a deep breath while leaning back against the chair. "*I was hoping it would be you . . ."* Her words lingered in his mind, bolstering his confidence and bringing a slight sense of intoxication.

He soon rose from his seat and set out for Cringle to work on his house. Eager to see Ruth, he could think of nothing better to do that would engage his mind and body and help the hours pass.

Earl swung a hammer, knocked out old cupboards and walls, and split firewood for the better part of the day, then returned to his parents' house to clean up. After having a quick bite to eat and jotting down a few notes in his journal about plans he had for his house, he walked with Danny down to the lake. Standing motionless with Danny sitting by his side, he stared into the calm waters and could see the slowly moving clouds reflected above, which brought a touch of peace to his anxious spirit. He was always fascinated by how the afternoon winds subsided with the onset of evening, leaving the water to turn to glass. Perhaps it was the consistency of this, the order it possessed, that he appreciated and unknowingly relied upon.

A few minutes later, he pulled himself away from the lake and ascended the trail, and he and Danny were again in the truck, motoring off down the driveway and onto the road heading northeast towards town. They eventually reached Main Street and went to the old country store, where he proudly bought a small, freshly wrapped bouquet of flowers that he deemed the most vibrant of those the store had to offer.

"That is a fine batch of flowers, Earl. I hope they serve you well," said Mr. Burke while closing the cash register. He had a good idea of where they were going but said nothing of it. In a small town, news travels quickly to even the furthest borders, and so a balance had to be found between talking with others and respecting their privacy. As the owner of a store where most of the town entered at some point during the week, some of whom had the gift of gossip and gab, Mr. Burke had learned this balance quite well.

"Thank you, Mr. Burke. I believe they will," Earl responded, keeping the details to himself. Earl held deep trust in this aged man, but he felt no one under the sun needed any details just yet. He departed and climbed back into the truck and drove down the road, soon crossing over the borders of town.

Like most stretches of road in this area, he found this drive to be visually stimulating. The wooded hills to his left and the rolling valleys and pastures to his right possessed an undying beauty. There were times where he would stop the truck and simply admire it all. But not on this journey. Soon he and Danny reached the stables where he saddled up Obie, carefully tucked the flowers in the saddlebag, and set out with his two friends for Ruth's.

"We're going to see a girl, my friend," said Earl to Obie while leaning forward to rub his head. He then squeezed the horse's lower belly with his legs, and the animal let out a faint snicker and began to trot down the ageless tree-lined trail. Earl's heartbeat increased, and he gave another squeeze to turn the trot into a canter. The sound of hooves beating the earth always invigorated him, and Obie, sensing his master's anticipation, rose to the occasion.

Fortunately, Danny's great speed and endurance did not fail him. He darted through the woods, bounding over logs and cutting between trees as he followed Earl and Obie. It was a workout for him, though, and he had to run efficiently in order to keep up. Despite the sacrifice, he was thrilled to come along.

The three males pressed on through the land at various speeds, crossing through forest and open, rolling fields.

Soon they reached the Benson house, and Earl's heart thumped at the sight of it. From a distance he noticed Ruth out on the porch sitting on the railing, looking out into the horizon with her long hair flowing down over her shoulders. Earl brought Obie to a slow walk, hoping to preserve the sight before him. She looked beautiful, dressed simply in jeans and a button-down flannel shirt.

When Ruth noticed Earl approaching, she stood and walked to the steps, then leaned against the railing and watched as the trio approached her. For a moment she wondered if she had stepped into a fairy tale.

Earl dismounted as Ruth descended the steps and came to him. As usual, she could sense an eagerness coming from him that she found adorable.

"You sure know how to make a grand entrance," she said with her signature warmth and charm as she rubbed Obie's head.

"It's a Timmings thing," he responded with a grin, then turned and went for his saddlebag. "I brought these for you," he said, gently handing her the bouquet.

Ruth's eyes widened. She lifted the flowers to her face and inhaled deeply, her eyes closing in delight.

"These are beautiful," she said when she opened her eyes. "Thank you, Earl."

The two walked inside so Ruth could put the flowers in a vase, and then proceeded to the barn and saddled up Samuel. Soon they were riding down the driveway together towards the trails Earl knew so well. Samuel was a little tense as this was all new to him, so they kept the ride as leisurely as they could.

The ride lasted just over two hours, but it felt like minutes to them both. Soon they arrived back at the barn, where they unsaddled the horses and then found Ruth's family awaiting their company around the campfire. To his chagrin, Earl had to leave early in order to beat the darkness, and once again he found himself in the saddle after saying goodbye to Ruth in her front yard.

The three companions set out and rode through dusk, admiring the sky that gradually grew darker while the stars began to grow brighter. Everything became much darker when the journey led them into the forest, and after just a few minutes, Earl decided to turn around and take the longer route along the road that allowed for more light and less anxiety for all of them.

Turning from the trail, he felt the urge to look over his shoulder. At that moment, he thought he saw a bright white flash, small as a dime but bright as a star, deep within the forest. Alert, he looked more closely for a minute. No more flashes, nothing out of the ordinary at all. Just the swiftly darkening woods. Shaking his head, he rode on.

For the remainder of the ride, Earl was powerless to dwell on anything other than the next time he would be with Ruth. And that time would be soon, followed by many more times, all of which would combine to create a summer that neither of them would ever forget.

June 6, 1942
From Ruth's journal

Though I can understand Mother and Father's concern, tonight's ride along Sunset Trail was wonderful. We set out after dinner and had no intention of being gone as long as we did, all caught up in the moment—captivated by the beauty of the forest and the way the sun flickered through the trees while descending into the west.

When we arrived to our destination, we watched it finish its course by setting over the lake. It was breathtaking.

Earl told me that this was one of his favorite spots. I can see why.

Mornings, afternoons, and evenings beyond count, people could see dust rising from behind Earl's horse or truck, usually moving quickly, as he made his way north to see his girl. For those who were aware of the budding romance, the sight of the two would often bring a smile and a wave of nostalgia. For others, it stirred up longings of their own.

Riding horseback to Ruth's always came with a bit of extra adventure for Earl because it involved crossing through Sawyer Hills—the rugged, hilly, and heavily wooded forest that stretched throughout the western side of Mountain and far beyond. Of course there were some roads that went through it, though the quickest route to Ruth's house was via the trails. Though Earl preferred caution when riding alone, there were times where he let Obie reveal his speed, especially when passing through the open glades, where the rising or setting sun was displayed in its full splendor.

Regardless of whether the journey was made by horse or truck, he always arrived at the gravel drive that would take him through the canopy of trees, where a pretty smile and angelic voice awaited him. Earl reveled in these journeys to Ruth's, which were trumped only by those that she joined him on. And there were many. Some were long, some short, and many in between.

Together they would journey through the wooded hills and fields, crossing through small streams and rivers. Ruth was an experienced rider, though she had never cantered up steep hills or crossed through streams before, and the thrill of it all was simply wonderful to her. A few times, she just couldn't help but laugh out loud or shout with joy.

Many evenings, Earl took Ruth on a ride down Sunset Trail. One of his favorites, it was a narrow trail that meandered through the forest and, in the evening, boasted a breathtaking view of the setting sun through the trees. The trail led to a campsite on a small lake that captured the sunset in a way that left one speechless. Few knew of this spot, but those who did treasured it.

On one occasion, Earl and Ruth lingered too long at the campsite, forgetting how quickly the sun can set and leave the woods dark and formidable. Though Ruth felt safe with Earl and was thrilled by the sense of adventure, Earl was keenly aware of the risks involved with riding through the dark and prayed under his breath for a safe return, all while keeping them moving at a brisk pace.

When they finally emerged from the woods, it was almost completely dark. All the lights were on in Ruth's home, and Earl saw her father staring out the window towards the barn.

"Earl, I don't need to tell you the dangers of riding in the dark—"

"I'm so sorry, sir. The time just got away from me. It will not happen again."

Accepting full responsibility for the error, Earl felt terrible as he stood on the porch about to leave, apologizing once more to her parents. As he walked away towards his horse to go home, head down in discouragement, Ruth came quietly out the front door, then ran to him and threw herself into his arms.

"Thank you, Earl. The ride was wonderful, as usual," she whispered into his ear. She then released him and ran back into the house, turning back briefly to give him one final wave and a smile before closing the door, further assuring him that all was okay.

From that point on, he kept careful watch on the clock and skies and returned Ruth home at fitting times.

Of course, the visits between them didn't go just one way. Ruth would travel to Earl's or meet him for lunch during the week while he was at work. She would often surprise him, bringing him food that she had prepared herself, and together they would take a short walk around the town or sit at the picnic table behind the shop.

Earl worked with some guys who were a little rough around the edges and was at first concerned that they might say something offensive. However, Ruth navigated the scene with ease and softened even some of the toughest characters with her brightness. They also knew that Earl had strength, and deep down they suspected he could quickly become fierce if they were to disrespect her in any way.

June 25, 1942
From Earl's journal

> Fireflies. How many times in my life I marveled over and admired them, though I have never been as thankful for them as I have been tonight.
>
> Surprisingly, they are one of the few flying creatures that Danny doesn't attack. Jumbo flies and bees he will seek to devour, though fireflies he sits and watches. Makes me wonder what's going through his mind.
>
> The feeling of her being that close to me was something I do not want to forget as I go to sleep tonight.

There were nights of driving into town for ice cream, Danny always sitting between them in the truck. However, he soon found himself with less space than he had enjoyed in the past.

Afterward they would return to Ruth's and sit on the bench for hours underneath the stars in the backyard. Inside, her family would laugh quietly when hearing "There's one!" or "Whoa, look at that!" coming from them after seeing a shooting star, or on one occasion, dancing northern lights.

Sometimes they'd bring a blanket out and lay it out near the bench, then lie down on their backs and simply look up in wonder for hours. Lying there, each would point in various directions while the other quickly looked in the direction of the other's finger. These skies would continue to speak to each of them after saying goodbye for the night, whether from the saddle, truck, or while peering out through the bedroom window before drifting off to sleep.

And it wasn't only the skies that lit up their souls. For whatever reason, it seemed there was an abundant population of fireflies that summer, one of Earl's favorite of all creations. Once, one landed right on Earl's forearm while they were sitting together on the bench, just blinking away for a few minutes before flying off.

"I wonder if he's trying to say something to us," Ruth whispered, leaning in close to Earl to admire it and then staying there for a time. Aside from their occasional hugs, it was the closest she had ever gotten to him—and neither of them was oblivious to this. Yet it would not lead to anything, for at one point early on in their acquaintance they shared their mutual stance on saving everything, even a kiss, for marriage. In both their minds, they knew something as innocent as a kiss, which they believed held great power, could produce a spark that was not yet ready to be harnessed.

But they could not deny the strong urge; the pull to come ever closer as each day passed, and the desire to enjoy the pleasures of intimacy that were not yet meant to be enjoyed. By faith and examples they had witnessed, they knew this desire could be held in check until the chosen time. Furthermore, they believed that by doing so, they would create a fire within that would one day grow into such a powerful flame that would endure all storms and trials in this life and keep them warm and satisfied until the end of their days on this earth. A flame full of great physical and emotional pleasure, unknown to those who chose immediate gratification despite consequences and ignore the purity and sanctity of that which was only intended to be enjoyed within the boundaries of marriage between a man and a woman.

July 10, 1942
From Ruth's journal

> I'm not a drinker, though today, late in the afternoon, I felt like I had been. We were at the river again, when the clouds moved in and rain began to fall with minimal warning. Earl waded in from the water in case of lightning, and together we walked downstream a stone's throw away and sat underneath the shelter of our favorite willow tree. The sounds of rushing water, rainfall hitting the trees, and Earl's voice reading poetry to me were simply intoxicating.

There were the afternoons and early evenings when they would sit along the bank of the river and talk of life, while the lush sounds of water running its course filled the air.

Sometimes Earl would fish while Ruth basked in solitude on a blanket on the grass, reading a book or writing in her journal. At times she would stop and admire the young man wading in the water, silently wondering what was to come, dreaming of those things that young women dream about. Yet she tried to hold onto those dreams loosely, knowing, to some degree, that life can reshape them in the blink of an eye.

Likewise, Earl would look over and appreciate the sight of this beautiful young woman looking so contented while reading her book, occasionally looking off into the distance in what he perceived to be a daydream. In a way he couldn't describe, in a way that was so completely new to him, he was thankful that he was able to provide a touch of joy and peace to this young woman by giving her time to herself along life-giving waters. That she had chosen to spend her time with him at all was a fact he was still unable to fully comprehend. For as humble and grounded as he was, there was something within him, and perhaps every man alive, which asks the question, *"Do I have what it takes?"*

Yet this young woman, who could have her pick of so many young men, was here with him.

Earl whispered more than one "Thank-you" up into the sky when considering this. Once, she caught the movement of his lips and asked him what he was saying.

"I'll tell you soon, though not today," he replied with a smile, feeling it was best to save these words for a bit and also deriving some enjoyment of putting her in suspense.

"Okay, then," she said coyly, looking back down to her book, then back up at him, "but know that I'll be watching." Earl laughed heartily at that, enjoying her strong, playful spirit, before going back to his fishing.

"I'll keep that in mind," he said, looking back at her as he prepared to cast.

On a few occasions, he would read poetry to her, sometimes poems he had written himself. One in particular came on a late, rainy afternoon while they sat on the river's edge under the protection of a willow tree:

> Maker of all things beautiful, let your
> light shine down upon these days.
> > Thank you for this special, long-haired
> > beauty, and all her wonderful ways.
> Bless our time together, please don't let it
> move by too fast,
> > Teach us to enjoy the morning, day,
> > and evening, the present and the past.

That summer also brought countless hours spent together on the lake, where Earl would row them along in no hurry whatsoever. Each time Danny would be sitting between them in the craft, slightly anxious, but comforted by Ruth as usual, so happy to be along.

Sometimes they went out in the early morning, when the fog still covered the water. A few times they lingered on the water into the afternoon, when the sun shone directly above them and became so hot that they jumped into the water to cool off. Ruth actually initiated this first, diving in unexpectedly. Earl, no stranger to lake swimming, followed her immediately. Time would pass into the late afternoon, where the sun began to descend and produce an immensely bright white trail of light on the lake's ripples.

Most often, they ventured onto the waters in the evenings, which would be their most cherished excursions, when the day slowed down and the skies over the lake were painted with bright shades of fiery pink and orange that never grew old or normal. Again, Earl would fish while Ruth read. Ruth also enjoyed fishing and Earl was an avid reader, though Ruth took it to another level and consumed literature in great amounts, delighting in being able to do so while this handsome man, who cherished her company, sat on the other end of the boat.

"Hmm," she said playfully, setting her book down for a minute on her lap. She was lying on the bench with her head resting on the gunwale, padded by a sweatshirt, "I don't see you catching many fish tonight. Lost your touch?"

"It sure seems that way . . ." he said calmly, his voice trailing off at the end. "Perhaps we need to move to a different spot and rouse the fish a little." He took the oars and began rowing in a sloppy, comical fashion that made her giggle, until she felt the first intentional splash of water on her face that caused her to jump up into sitting position.

"Hey!" she shouted in surprise.

"That should do it," he said, returning to his fishing position wearing a proud smile.

"Oh, you're in for it mister," she said laughing, wiping the dripping water from her face.

In between it all were countless walks together, long drives through the countryside, visits to his house in Cringle so he could proudly show her his progress, helping one another's family with projects around the house, aiding others in the community by delivering supplies or assisting with building projects, and helping with the children on Sunday mornings.

Along the way, a new addition entered the scene that added even more zest to their times together: a chunky, shiny-coated black lab puppy that the Bensons purchased from a family on the other side of town. Steven, after repeated exposure to Danny, couldn't hold back. They named him Benny, and his sweet, gregarious personality quickly won their hearts. Danny took to the new dog quickly also, forming a deep affection and taking up an older-brother role.

And they danced. Like the wind sailing over the waters or swirling around leaves in the fall, they danced. Through the heat of summer, into the freshness of fall, and into the sharp bite of winter, whether in their backyards, the middle of town, or a venue in a far-off city where Tom was playing guitar, they danced.

September 20, 1942
From Earl's journal

"Don't rush these times son. Enjoy the beauty and thrill found in them, and remember that both good and hard times are waiting for you down the road of life. And while we are not to be consumed by this truth, we should take heed. At the end of pondering such matters, remember who gave you this life, and do your best to enjoy it one day at a time, making good with what you've been given."

Dad wrote these words to me the other morning while he was at work. We had a good talk the night before while fly-fishing, where I shared some thoughts about Ruth. As I sit here down by the waters, his words continue to speak to me. I have no reason to doubt that they are pure wisdom that he acquired through the years, and I intend to write them on my heart and live them out all my days.

I am thankful for that man.

As Earl and Ruth's relationship continued to grow, they became even more inseparable. Lively debates, healthy arguments, sweet reconciliations, genuine tears, and rich laughter followed them everywhere they went. Both mature beyond their years, with wise counsel never far away and soft hearts willing to heed it, their journey together progressed more rapidly than most.

But as with most young romances, their time together would not be without challenge. And a great challenge was on their doorsteps—one that would forever reshape all their hopes and dreams.

Winter Tears

January 17, 1943
From Ruth's journal

He leaves tomorrow, and I feel I have no strength to offer in this time of need. Part of me feels so selfish, as if my dreams for the future are more important than all else. Another part of me is concerned for his very life, and for this I feel no shame.

God, please strengthen my heart for this, and forgive this intense anger I feel for what is going on. I don't want him to go, but if that is the way this story is to be written, then I do not want to get in the way.

Ruth stood motionless by the window. Every part of her body felt numb, and the only comfort she felt came from her mother's arms that were wrapped around her as she wept.

Since the United States had joined the war a year ago, young men from around the country, mainly between the ages of eighteen and twenty-six, were leaving their homes and loved ones and being sent to basic training or boot camp before being shipped overseas. And now the day that Ruth had hoped would not come was now upon her: Earl would soon be among those leaving home.

"I knew it was possible," she said in a broken voice, "though inside I wouldn't allow myself to believe that it would actually happen."

"I know honey, I know," said her mother softly. "I'm not sure any girl could."

Up until this day she had remained composed and steady, anchored by her reliance on Providence. And while her moorings had remained firmly intact, the force of the crashing waves was simply overwhelming. She looked out the window that faced the pond and the bench before it, as well as the vast yard that surrounded it. What was once green, vibrant, and living now lay barren and frozen in the winter chill. The deadness of it all, combined with Earl's imminent departure, seemed almost too much to bear, especially as she looked upon the places where the two of them spent many special times together.

"Oh God," she softly cried, "must he go?"

Her mother's heart ached for her daughter as she stood holding her. Her father walked over and laid his hand on her shoulder, and he too felt the weight of not being able to do anything to take away his little girl's pain.

The news had come to Earl that cold winter's day in early January while at work. The mailman, Ronald, would sometimes drop into the shop to deliver mail directly to Earl in order to save himself a trip to their house. As Earl flipped through the letters, he stopped at one addressed to himself and opened it. Seeing the salutation, he stood silent and motionless.

"Greeting: You are hereby ordered . . ."

From previous stories of other young men being summoned to war, mostly those a few years younger than himself, Earl knew what this meant. It was a conscription letter that signified his induction into the military. He had been drafted.

Later, he would reflect upon how he had often heard people say how they had a hundred different thoughts flash through their mind at certain points in their life. For when he had read that letter, he experienced that very same thing.

Thankfully, Ruth did not surprise him by coming to visit him at work this day, as she was out of town with her father until that evening. Earl groaned inwardly at the thought of having to tell her the news. Their days up until now had been ever growing in excitement, and the implications of this news seemed like a giant hammer crashing down on it all.

He quietly folded the letter, looked out the window from where sunlight poured in, and closed his eyes. He then walked to the restroom, shut the door behind him, and dropped to his knees, desperate for strength.

When he rose, he went to his boss to inform him of the letter. Somber but encouraging, his boss offered him the rest of the day off, though Earl felt it would be better to continue working to allow him to process the weight of it all before going home to share the news with his family.

He did get a surprise visit from Tom shortly after lunch, and discovered that he too received the same letter that day. They went for a walk together down the road, warmed by the sun shining on their faces while the harsh January wind bit at their skin.

"Well, brother, I think we both knew deep down that this hour was coming," said Tom.

"I know. There's just something different between thinking something big might be coming—and holding it in your hands," replied Earl, looking down at the letter as they walked along. "This is . . . heavy."

They talked about how they were going to tell the others, and discussed whether they would have voluntarily enlisted if they hadn't received these letters from the president. Both acknowledged that, under the circumstances, considering all they had been hearing, they would have. They found no thrill at the idea of going off to battle as so many other young men they knew seemed to feel, since they were more aware of the realities of war due to their father's experiences. And they thought long and hard about what they would be leaving behind. Nonetheless, they felt it right to go, and in some sense, this eased the burden of choosing to enlist.

"Earl, I'd like to share the news together with you. I can come by the shop after work and we can drive to the house together, if you don't mind."

"No, I don't mind at all. Seems the best thing to do."

"Okay, brother. I'll see you in a few hours."

That evening, after Tom and Earl arrived back at their parents' house, they asked that everyone gather around the kitchen table. Their tone was marked by an unmistakable graveness, and they wasted little time in sharing the news. There was no laughter, no teasing, no talk of fishing. Instead, a deep solemnity hung in the air.

Then they talked. For hours they shared their feelings about what was to come. Patricia's eyes were wet and fresh tears frequently emerged. Little Stephanie was sad too, even though she could not fully grasp the seriousness of the situation, or the possibility that when her two big brothers went away, they might not return.

Richard remained composed. He felt it was his responsibility to be an anchor for the family this night. A great storm surged in his soul, though, and under his breath was a constant stream of prayers for strength, for he knew better than all where his sons were going and the horror that lay waiting for them. And he also felt the helplessness of knowing that his family was in harm's way, and there was nothing in his power he could do to stop it.

But this evening ended in a quiet triumph. The family prayed together and talked of how Tom and Earl could make a difference over there. It was by no means a time of celebration but rather a time of digging deep and looking directly ahead with courage and purpose, not denying fear but exposing it to something greater.

As the family discussion came to a close, Earl again felt the enormous weight of what he had to do next: tell the girl he adored with all his heart that he would soon be leaving her.

Earl and Danny climbed into the pickup and began the drive to Ruth's. He drove slowly, his mind bending in so many different directions as he tried to figure out the best way to tell her. She already knew that he had something important to say, from the serious tone he used when he called her, though this would undoubtedly hit her with more force than anything else she could imagine. And yet, with all the other young men in the region being called into service, he wondered if she might be expecting it.

Earl pulled up the driveway and saw Ruth emerge from the door and walk to the truck to greet them. She wore a soft smile that made his heart ache even more.

They gave each other a hug and went inside, and after briefly greeting her family, who were all sitting around the living room, they went into the den and sat by the fireplace. Preparing to tell her the news, Earl looked to the ground with strained eyes as he tried to find the words, and when he lifted his head he saw her looking at him with concerned eyes that pierced his soul.

"Ruth, I received this in the mail today," he said, pulling the letter from his pocket and presenting it to her. She looked at the letter then back up at him, and then cautiously took it from him. Slowly, she unfolded the paper and began to read. Earl could see the life in her eyes progressively diminish. "I'm so sorry."

Despite the cold of winter, Earl and Ruth went for many walks together in those following days. They drank deeply of each other's company, despite being constantly followed by the shadow that would soon separate them. They walked along the river, listening to its comforting sounds. They went on several horseback rides through the forest. They served together at the hospital and other places in the community. They sat before the fireplace and read to each other. But mostly, they just talked.

One step at a time, Ruth and Earl learned how to continue living even in the midst of trying times. Though there were moments along the way where the walls of reality seemed to close in around them, their resolve to press forward grew daily.

One of those moments came when the two of them were walking through downtown Mountain just before dark, as light, fluffy snow fell all around them.

"Ruth, we've talked briefly about this already," he went silent for a moment searching for the right words, "but from what I understand, guys who enter this war do not come back until it's over." Or injured, he reflected, if at all, but he could not say this to her. "And there's no way of knowing how long it will last. If you—" he stopped again, looking up into the sky then back at the ground, and from the corner of his eye he could feel her powerful gaze upon him, hanging on his words. "If it gets too hard, if too much time passes, I don't expect you to wait—"

It was at that precise moment when Earl felt a surprisingly swift and formidable blow to his rib cage delivered by a hand that he did not know possessed such force.

"Earl Timmings!" she yelled, now standing just inches in front of him with eyes of pure fire that were staring directly into his, bringing their walk to a dead stop. Earl could feel his body tighten, as if preparing for another decisive blow at any moment. "Don't ever say those words again!" And with that, another blow did come.

A few tears fell from her eyes, though her fierceness was unrelenting. She stood there staring at him, searching his eyes for a moment in silence, and what she found was sincere agreement. "I will be here for you when you return," she said while shoving him in the chest with both hands, causing him to take a step back. "I will be here waiting—promise me you will never forget these words, Earl. Promise me!"

"I promise," Earl said in a gentle, broken voice, taken back by her emotion and loyalty. "I will never say those words again." Earl generally felt a danger in using the word "never," but he felt no caution in saying it now.

Ruth's raging fire subsided to a candle flame, and she moved in to his embrace. There on the side of the street, they held each other for a long moment while the snow, illuminated by the street light that grew as night darkened, continued to fall softly all around them.

Like every chapter in life that is lived to the fullest, those days before Earl's departure passed quickly. Soon Earl found himself standing in front of his suitcase making final preparations the night before leaving. When finished, he and Danny climbed in the truck and began the journey to Ruth's house.

Of all the visits in recent weeks, including the first one to tell her the news, this one was by far the heaviest to bear. Even watching Danny jump into the truck was heart-wrenching. Danny was somehow different, and Early knew that his loyal friend could sense something was about to happen.

"Will you remember me, friend, if I am gone long?" he said while looking into the dog's eyes as they drove down the road. Danny's response was gentler than Ruth's; he simply looked deeply and lovingly into his master's eyes and put his head in his face while casually wagging his tail. Earl's eyes swelled, and he wondered what would come of Danny if he were not to return. But he fought it off and put his arm around his friend as they continued their journey.

Steven opened the door when Earl arrived and greeted him warmly. He showed him in to the kitchen, where he and his wife spoke with him for a few moments before indicating that Ruth was in the other room.

"She's expecting you."

Earl nodded and thanked them, then walked slowly into the den, where Ruth sat quietly by the fireplace. When she heard him come in, she wiped some tears from her eyes and stood up to face him, trying earnestly to conceal her grief with a courageous smile.

Earl saw this and walked directly to her and embraced her tightly. Immediately, she began to sob in his shoulder. A single tear slipped down Earl's cheek, then another, and he had to dig deep to stay strong at a time when he felt he must.

"God knows, Ruth . . ." he whispered into her ear. "I'll do everything I can to come back to you."

She cried softly and buried her face in his chest, and he just held her there in front of the fire with his chin resting gently on her head. She said nothing, but just held him tighter.

Few words were spoken the rest of the evening. Before Earl left, they all sat together at the kitchen table to pray, and again a sense of hope overcame the shadow in their hearts.

Driving home with a heavy heart, Earl passed a vast snow-covered field that he'd seen a thousand times. Yet tonight, it sat glowing in the moonlight with such an overpowering beauty and serenity that he felt forced to pull over onto the side of the road. He turned off the truck and the lights and stepped out of the truck, motioning for Danny to join him.

Earl walked to the edge of the road and stood looking into the white wonderland that stretched for miles. He then looked down at Danny, who sat at his feet, the reality again setting in that this could be one of their last nights together for a very long time, possibly forever.

"You've been so good to me, friend," he said while gently petting Danny's head, then slowly sat down on the frozen ground next to him. "I'll do my best to come back for you. But you won't be alone, because Ruth is going to be spending a lot of time with you," he said in a shaky voice. At that moment, Danny lifted one paw and placed it on Earl's shoulder, and it was at that moment Earl broke down and began to weep.

Richard slept sparingly that night, rolling quietly out of his bed more than once to fall on his knees. With barely a whisper, he asked one more time if there was any other way. Finally, though, he released completely his desire to rewrite the story, and instead asked for safety for his boys. Things were put into motion that could not be undone.

Before returning to bed, he walked to the wood stove in the family room and added a couple logs, though it was really the peace and power of the fire he had come for. With only hours before the departure, he quietly returned to his bedroom and knelt again, praying for strength and courage, not only for himself but for his family, to be given them this next morning. When he believed no more could be said or asked for, he gently climbed back into bed and fell quickly asleep next to his wife, whose emotional exhaustion left her in a sound sleep.

In the other room, Earl, like his father, slept sparingly. Several times throughout the night he slipped out of bed and walked to the window to stare out into the woods, where the radiant moonlight sent shadows to the ground all around. He also made a trip to the wood burner once, just an hour before his father did, to be comforted by the heat and flames that danced on the ceiling and walls. He returned to bed and lay on his back, praying quietly, mainly for Ruth, who seemed to be holding much inside as of late in an effort to be strong.

Just miles away, Tom was also standing before the fire at his house, preparing his heart for what was to come, occasionally looking out the window and being comforted by the landscape. This night, he thought to himself, made life—with all its responsibilities, relationships, opportunities, and twists and turns—seem more precious and fleeting than ever before. His dad often talked about how quickly life moves by and how it comes with few guarantees and a lot of surprises, and now he understood in more depth the truth of those words.

Early the next morning, those close to Earl and Tom had come to see them off, and it was no small number of people. Richard had volunteered to drive them south, together with some other young men from the town, to the train depot where their journey to boot camp would begin. Though nobody looked forward to that moment where the goodbyes had to be said, there was a surprising air of calm and peace that held everyone together that morning. Fear and grief was overcome by providence. Eyes were moist and sniffles were numerous, though the flood of tears had already passed and had yielded to the reality that all was out of their hands.

Ruth and Ann were among those with tear-stained cheeks, though Ruth possessed a sense of quiet strength that Earl noticed immediately that morning—a quiet strength and determination that he would remember many times in the days to come.

Before they left, Richard humbly called them together to pray together one final time before leaving. They all came in close and formed a circle, and Richard's was the final voice before they closed and let the morning run its course.

"Father," he spoke with a humble, steady voice, "thank you for these young men, and please be with them every step, and bring them home safe. Use them over there, and let your light shine brightly in their hearts when all the lights seem to be out everywhere else. Your will be done."

Final hugs were given, long and with few words. Earl's final embrace was with Ruth, who gave him a small silver locket attached to a chain.

"I've had this since I was a young girl. I remember being fascinated by how strongly the sunlight reflected off of it. Please take it with you."

Earl gently took the locket and opened it. Inside, she'd placed a picture of herself standing next to a horse, wearing a smile on her face so beautiful that tears welled in his eyes.

"Thank you, Ruth," he said, then looked back up at her. "This will never leave my side."

Right before Earl was to enter the car, he took one final look back at her. Without words, he gave her a smile that spoke confidence and tenderness, then turned away and stepped in the car.

For those close to these young men, the rest of the day would be one of the longest they would ever experience, and the whole town seemed to be silenced. Reports of the war and loss of life had reached them, and they knew the risks involved. But for those who recognized this life as a temporary dwelling, hope would continually rise above the darkness that tried to overcome their souls, and together, they would endure.

Separated by Sea

Dear Earl,

The following collection of letters and journal entries you're about to read were difficult to compile, for obvious reasons. You leaving for the war and those long days that followed are vivid memories full of so much pain and anguish. It is undeniable, though, that those times brought such immense growth and shaping for the both of us.

I will never forget saying goodbye to you that morning and watching the car drive away.

Earl leaned back and folded the small note that Ruth had attached to a stack of letters. On the outside of the note she had written, "Separated by Sea." He took a sip of coffee and opened the first envelope to begin the journey into a dimly lit period of their past.

January 20, 1943—Heading west through the night
From Earl's journal

With the sound of the train rumbling down the tracks, a part of me wonders if I am yet to come out of a daydream. Have the recent events really taken place? The letters that both Tom and I received from the President on that snowy afternoon, having to say goodbye to home and family just weeks later, then boarding this train for boot camp . . . it's all hard to grasp right now. And soon we'll be climbing aboard a ship that will carry us to an unknown destination where we will fight against an adversary of whom we know so little.

The sound of Tom snoring softly in the seat across from me seems to dispel any possibility that this is just a dream.

I will never forget the feeling of reading that letter, nor of sitting around the table with the family the night that we shared the news. Seeing Mom's tears and imagining the grief she must have felt was almost unbearable. And Dad, who held steady but whose heavy eyes could not conceal grief of his own. I can only imagine what it must be like as a father, having to be strong for a wife and kids in those circumstances. Having been through a war himself, I believe there is much he has seen that he has not revealed to us, and probably for good reason.

I am so thankful for him, for them both.

What has settled in my memory the most, though, is the look on Ruth's face as she read the induction letter. The dismay that shown from her eyes was unmistakable, and again, there was nothing I could do about it. Nothing. I know she was trying to be strong and unselfish, but this time I could see through her. It made my heart ache, especially knowing that I was the cause of this pain.

And I can't help but wonder: will she wait for me? Will she be there for me when I return? I feel guilty even considering this question, for she is as solid and resolute a young woman as I have ever met, and she's never given any hint of uncertainty. The bruise on my chest from her punching me serves as evidence.

Though how resolute can one remain if years, multiple years, were to pass? I have already determined in my heart that nothing on either side of the ocean, save death, will stop me from pursuing her. Yet it is my understanding that soldiers will not be returning from this battle until it is over, unless badly injured or killed, neither of which are favorable alternatives. Will she hold out? Can I expect her to?

It is obvious that I cannot trust or lean on my own understanding at this point. Too much remains hidden behind future's veil.

And then there is the ring . . .

January 21, 1943
From Earl's journal

Our train stopped in North Platte, Nebraska on our journey west, and we were welcomed by volunteers, mostly women, who had a hot cup of coffee for us and all kinds of homemade sweets and sandwiches. Fittingly, the place is called the North Platte Canteen, and it was there that I received one of the warmest and most generous greetings I had ever received in all my life. They gave us hugs, forced more food on us than we felt we deserved, and encouraged us to stay strong and brave. They made us feel appreciated, and I'm not sure one soldier, whether the most hard-hearted or terrified, did not step back on that train without feeling his heart lifted. Thank you, North Platte.

The train rumbled through the Midwest and into the western frontier, and it was the first time Earl had seen that part of the country. Though he preferred the lakes, rivers, and woods of Wisconsin, the mountains and prairies impressed him. The knowledge of where they were going slightly obscured the beauty of it all, though, and hung over the camaraderie of some of the young men like a great, dark cloud that was waiting to burst with torrential rains. Some acted as though they were on their way to a sporting event, singing and carrying on in merriment, either oblivious to the rigors and horror of war or determined to face it with bravado. Despite anything they had heard and regardless of training, however, all of the soon-to-be soldiers on the train were completely unaware of just how heavy that cloud's downfall would actually be once they stepped into the Pacific theater.

Nonetheless, Earl and Tom felt an inner strength rooted deep within that would sustain them through all their days, from the train ride to boot camp and to what lay beyond. Though not immune from the weight of it all, they continued to radiate light, courage, and integrity and were a source of strength and hope to many others. Even some of the most vile and arrogant of boys who had yet to reveal a hint of actual manhood, and there were plenty, could not help but restrain their immature conduct when in their presence. And a few of them were not the same after.

When he wasn't talking with others, Earl could be found sitting in his seat gazing out the window at all that passed by. His mind was both relaxed and engaged by the vast rolling plains where herds of buffalo grazed in the distance, dwarfed by the backdrop of the massive, snow-peaked Rocky Mountains that sat unwavering in the distance. He would stare thoughtfully at the rivers, streams, and forests that passed, where scenes of home—and especially Ruth—would come to mind and linger long after the scene had passed. Sometimes a deep groan, filled with longing, would emerge from him during those moments, and he would simply close his eyes and seek comfort for his aching heart.

"What are you thinking about, brother?" asked Tom when hearing one of them.

"Walking along the river's edge with Ruth, and fishing with you and Dad, and Mom preparing our catch for dinner, and Stephanie getting upset with you for trying to steal her dessert," he replied wistfully after a short pause, his eyes never leaving the countryside that rolled past. "But more than anything, walking along the river's edge with Ruth."

Tom sighed reverently and leaned his head back into the seat, then looked out the window to indulge in his own quiet reflection.

"That is a fine daydream," he said tenderly.

For a moment, neither brother said a word as they looked out the window, where all they could see were glimpses of their homeland and shadows of the unknown that lay ahead.

"Stephanie always was an easy one to ruffle up," said Tom with a warm smile, breaking the silence.

"And you were always gifted in doing so," said Earl, laughing. The two fell silent again.

"We have a long journey ahead, Earl. Let's hold fast."

Many long, candid conversations ensued with his brother and a few others who came close to them during those times. Tom and Earl always enjoyed one another's openness, though it seemed to be taken to a deeper level since this journey began—perhaps because they both knew there was a reasonable chance that one or the both of them would not be returning home. Though they had both directly confronted this fact in their hearts, the thought remained something that neither of them was ready to share with the other. But they knew, and it made them appreciate one another more than ever.

They eventually reached the west coast, and when the train stopped at the station, a whistle blew and another train full of would-be soldiers stood up and gathered their belongings. The two brothers looked at one another and nodded. They were now one step closer.

Boot camp was completed in just under six weeks—more rapidly than normal due to the escalating war campaign and the military's need for more troops. During their time there, Tom and Earl proved their capabilities with firearms and combat and quickly gained respect as valuable, trustworthy soldiers who knew how to both lead and submit to the leadership above them. Not that they weren't tested and chiseled by the extreme rigor and intensity of the training, though it was obvious that the training was only improving upon an already established foundation.

Now forged for battle, the two young men and their comrades boarded a huge passenger-cargo liner now serving as a troop transport ship that would carry them into action. Just weeks before, it had been transporting fruit from Central America; now it was transporting these young men to an uncertain fate. Everything was happening so fast that they felt they were caught up in a whirlwind, yet they held steady and kept their gaze forward.

Dear Earl,

You left for the war today, and words can't express how I feel. Know that you will be in my thoughts and prayers constantly, and most assuredly my dreams as well.

You have given me so much joy over the past year. Enough, I believe, to fuel my heart with light in the dark days that are sure to emerge during the time that we are apart. I promise I will spend lots of time with Danny and even take him out on the water as often as I can. I trust he will be a comfort to me and the rest of the family.

You fight to stay alive over there, Earl, for all of us. We want you both home, but we also desire for you to make a difference. I have little idea of what lies on a battlefield, or in the times between the fighting, but I know you are strong and brave and will do what is right. I'm so proud of you for the attitude you had during the entire time before your departure, right up until the time you left.

I love you, and please come home soon.

Your girl,
Ruth

Earl read the letter that misty morning while standing on the deck of the ship as the sun rose in the east. He had received it from her shortly after arriving at boot camp weeks earlier, and like every letter from Ruth, he read it so many times he had it memorized.

Earl gently folded the slightly worn letter and put it in his pocket, where it would remain until the next one arrived. As he closed the flap to the pocket and secured the button, he lifted his head to see the fading shoreline of the west coast and recalled the first time hearing Ruth speak the words *I love you* to him.

They were walking through the woods in late fall, shortly after the Bensons purchased Benny, who was bounding clumsily through the woods, trying earnestly to keep up with Danny, which was of course no use whatsoever.

"I love that boy," Earl said about Danny while hand in hand with Ruth. It was slightly challenging to hold hands in the woods, with all the obstacles and rugged terrain, but this was one of those days where it just felt right despite the mild inconvenience. "He runs through these woods with reckless abandon, checks on us every thirty seconds and comes back to play with the new guy. He seems to get younger with each passing year, so happy and alive."

"I think that has something to do with how his owner treats him and looks after him," said Ruth warmly, causing Earl to squeeze her hand a little tighter. Just then, Danny stopped to look back at them, his eyes glued on his master, who made a playful growling noise that made Danny crouch down with his hind end in the air, tail wagging, then take off again. Benny tried to follow but seemed to trip over every branch and stump in the process, making Earl and Ruth laugh every time.

"Ruth," said Earl, walking closer to her and turning his head to look at her.

Ruth slowed and looked at him, her curiosity all of a sudden heightened by his serious tone.

"I love you." Ruth's eyes grew heavy. "With all my heart and in a way I've never before experienced, I love you." Earl swallowed hard. "I am bona fide crazy about you."

Ruth swallowed hard and took a step towards him.

"And I, Earl Timmings, in a way that is altogether new to me, love you too."

As soon as the words reached his ears, Earl found himself at a loss for his own, and Ruth could feel his already gentle demeanor towards her soften even more, while his grip on her hand became firmer.

Ruth took a deep breath and threw herself into his arms, burying her head in his chest. Long before this day, Earl had shown his love for her without words; nonetheless, hearing it now had a dizzying effect on her. She would eternally hold onto those words and keep them close to her heart.

Now, with the great sea in front of him and the war machine churning and drawing him in, he held her words close to his heart, where they would remain.

Slow Drops of Rain

July 12, 1943
From Ruth's journal

He has been gone nearly seven months now. To say that I miss him any less than the first day would be a lie, though thankfully the intensity of the pain has lessened. But there are those days, those moments, where the angst is so deep, the desire to ask "why" so overpowering.

As they so often do, these mornings bring renewed hope. I wake and go to my knees where life fills my soul, refreshing my spirit and allowing me to see beyond the unknown. And for better or worse, the message comes that today may be the day that I learn of his return.

But as the day progresses, that hope seems to fade, and at times a thick haze seems to cover over everything. And it is in those moments when all seems lost, when every good thing in life seems to be overrun, that I cry out for help, and though my eyes may not see anything, my heart is provided with a small glimpse of light that provides me with just enough strength to keep going.

I also have to remember to look outside myself. I am not the first young woman to have

> her boyfriend leave for war, and in many ways our situation is so much less painful than others that I know. There are women with children, pressed down by challenging financial circumstances, whose provider is across the ocean, with no way of knowing if they are even alive apart from occasional letters.
>
> Those last words were hard to write.
>
> Though I know I must keep taking the day and blessing others in my path, I sometimes feel that I cannot carry the pain that comes with his absence. And the pain is especially strong on this beautiful midsummer's day, where the drops of rain seem to fall so slowly, as if they themselves are sad and faint-hearted. I know that we grow through pain and trials, though I confess that today I feel my patience is so fragile. I want him to be home, safe.
>
> God, please watch over him.

The day Earl left was the hardest day Ruth had ever experienced up to that point in her young life. After watching the car drive away, she returned to her house where she felt powerless to do anything but lie on her bed, tears streaming down her face while looking out the window. Within, she knew that she would not remain this way forever, but just then she could see no light and find no joy, but only hold on to the fact that she knew they existed and would one day return to her.

For hours she lay, relatively motionless, getting up sparingly to go for short walks, then return. A few times her mother came in to console her, speaking few words, crying with her while gently running her hand over her head.

Through sleep, dream, and sorrow, Ruth would pass through the day. A day in which time seemed to stand painfully still.

But strength and hope would rescue her the next morning, and she would remember that the sun always rises.

Ruth was always one for walking, though never so much as since Earl's departure. Her parents would watch with heavy hearts as she would put on her shoes and announce that she was going to step out for a while, knowing immediately from the tone of her voice how her spirit was doing. Benny would often follow along jubilantly, always a faithful provider of joy.

Regardless of how she felt, Ruth was determined to not let circumstances rule her days. She also resisted the urge to run from the occasional anguish or deny the challenge of it all. She believed, as truly as someone her age could, that trials, which come to all people in one way or another, are no excuse for curling up and giving in. Furthermore, she knew trials bring growth to those who choose to face them head-on. Responsibilities remain, opportunities to bless exist, and if she was able to refresh other people with her life, she believed that same refreshment would come back to her. Regardless, it was just the right thing to do.

Ruth continued to volunteer in the community, frequently visiting with elderly and helping out at an orphanage at the edge of town. She remained active in the church, spending time with the children and shining as an example for some of the other young women. She also made it a priority to spend time with other women whose husbands were inducted into the war, especially those who received news that their men would not be coming home. Her heart would ache for days after those encounters, and it was only by her faith and the support of others in her own life that she was able to hold steady through it all.

Nonetheless, everyone, no matter how unselfish and responsible, breaks down at times from the seemingly unbearable weight of life. And Ruth, a young woman with vibrant dreams and struggles of her own, was one of them.

On those dark days, when all hope seemed to have fled, she turned to her bedroom. She would always rise again, though, lifted by a hand other than her own that enabled her to press on.

She began taking nursing classes—something she had dreamed of doing for years. Earl had encouraged and supported her greatly in this, and she believed there were so many ways she could make a difference with this training. The years ahead would prove her correct.

Perhaps her favorite thing to do in these times, though, was to roam freely through the woods with Danny and Benny, and to spend time with Earl's parents, Stephanie, and Ann. There was an obvious comfort to be found in their company since they were enduring the absence of the same people, and the times together were sweet and comforting. Many nights they shared dinner, often with Ruth's parents, too, further deepening the family relationships. And on numerous occasions, Danny would come home with Ruth to spend the night at the Bensons', where he would find his way up onto Ruth's bed to snuggle.

"I'm glad you don't know where your master is," Ruth spoke to Danny as she fell asleep.

Though Danny certainly was unaware of where Earl was, he knew something was amiss. A smart, keen dog, he would perk up whenever he heard Earl's name spoken and study the face of the person from whose mouth it came. He could often be seen waiting expectantly by the entrance to the house for Earl to come home, or by his bedroom door, his head resting on his paws with sad but hopeful eyes. More than once, Ruth had found Danny sitting in the back of Earl's truck, as if he was remembering old rides. For those who had known the dog over the years, they could see a change in him with Earl being away—a slightly subdued bounce to his step. He was still social and friendly, however, and a source of consistent comfort to both families.

No matter the occasion, or whether the day was full of sun or clouds, Ruth would wonder how Earl was doing. Embracing the reality that he could be dead or wounded was something that no young woman could fully do, yet she had to carry this with her every moment of every day. And she'd often look to the west when the sun was setting, believing in her heart that somewhere far off in the Pacific, in a strange land beyond the Midwest, the Great Plains, and Rocky Mountains, her man was alive.

May 4, 1943
From Earl's journal

After being in the shadows of this war for months, our first battle experience came today. I now understand how charged a man's blood can become within him when advancing forward despite unparalleled fear. Yet the ugliness of it all, the sights and sounds of wounded and dying men, whether on our side or against us, far outweighs the satisfaction of any glory that could possibly come from all this. The details of what I saw, and felt, are beyond my capacity to write.

Honor can be fitting and war is sometimes necessary, but glory . . . I just don't see it.

Tom and Earl's first experience of battle came to them one morning on an island in the South Pacific. The fighting was fierce at times, and not without casualties. Both of them had the blood of their comrades on their clothes. Yet unknown to them it was only a small taste of the fighting that was to come.

After the operation was complete, the weary soldiers were taken to their base camp on a nearby island, Pavavu, where they would recuperate for a time while the American military continued to strengthen its force. Preparations were being made for continued island-hopping campaigns that would push them closer to the Japanese mainland where an imminent, climactic invasion was being planned.

Some days passed quickly, others lagged, and the inhospitable terrain of the island and near-constant rain was of no comfort to the soldiers, many of whom became sick. Days, weeks, and months would pass, and before they knew it, a year had expired when the soldiers could sense something in the air—a shift of momentum, a movement of personnel and equipment, discussions among officers—and they all knew what this meant.

Soon they were climbing back into a transport ship and heading further east to an island named Peleliu, and after days of passing through seemingly endless waters, they saw land in the distance. As if on command, every soldier's pulse quickened at the sight.

Hours passed like minutes, and soon they were within striking distance. The flashing red lights in the belly of the ship signaled to the troops that it was time to load into the amtracs that would carry them to shore. The large door of the ship opened, and the soldiers shielded their eyes from the intensely bright sunlight suddenly pouring into the dark loading area.

Earl and his company motored through the turbulent waters towards the small island. Theirs was one of scores of other amphibious assault vehicles. The sight was both awesome and terrible: hundreds of war vessels dotting the ocean and advancing into what some would later call hell. Tom was in one of the crafts, not far from Earl, but Earl had lost sight of him when his amtrac launched. What neither of them knew was that it would go on to be one of the most violent confrontations in the entire Pacific front.

As they motored on, bullets began screaming by and bombs exploded all around them, sending splashes of water over the sides of the armored craft. Far off, but getting closer each second, was the shoreline of the island. It was like a censer, pouring out smoke that rose high into the air. The sight was so horrifying and overwhelming that some of the soldiers around Earl began to vomit, overwhelmed by the magnitude of the situation.

The amtracs eventually reached the shore and crawled out of the water onto the sand. Some were forced to stop short and unload into the shallow water, as other amtracs had taken up all the space on the beach. One by one the soldiers flung themselves over the sides of the fortified boat, some taking their last breath as bullets picked them off before they even hit the surface. The water around the crafts began to take on a reddish hue from the American blood it was absorbing.

Earl jumped over and splashed into the water, gasping for air as his head surfaced. He immediately began pushing his way to shore, then fell to his stomach and crawled his way up the beach. Following his unit as best he could, he meandered through, and sometimes over, dead bodies that were strewn along the sand. The whole time, bullets continued to stream over and around him. He was like a machine now, thinking of nothing but survival. Ahead of him, he saw an impromptu bunker, a large hole in the ground created by an aerial bomb, where other men in his unit had grouped together before advancing further. A few strides later, he dove into the bunker with reckless abandon. Seconds later, a shell impacted the ground he had just covered, obliterating his footsteps in the sand.

For days they advanced, though much more slowly and with many more casualties than the intelligence had anticipated. The Japanese, strategically fortified within the cave systems they developed in the hills and steep ridges of the island, were an enemy that did not believe in the idea of surrender. The concept and ideology of this act was as disgusting to them as these American soldiers who were invading their land. And the island itself, with its rocky, ashen terrain and intense tropical heat, offered no mercy.

Initially, it was estimated that they'd achieve success within days.

In actuality, they would be there for months. And it was there that the horror of war would be forever burned into Earl's life.

"Timmings! Get over here!"

Earl took his eyes off the terrain in front of him and looked to his left, where someone was yelling for him with such ardency.

"It's your brother!"

Without hesitation, Earl rushed from his position, running as quickly as he could while trying to stay low under the cover of rock and brush. He recognized Jimmy, a sandy-haired kid no more than eighteen. "Follow me!" he said, and Earl nodded. The two ran for a short distance before the brush yielded a group of wounded soldiers.

And there was Tom, lying on his back, breathing heavily and in obvious great pain. His chest was covered in blood.

Earl dropped to his knees next to him and grabbed hold of Tom's hand. A sense of horror rushed over him. "Tom!"

He could feel Tom's grip tighten around his, an acknowledgment of Earl's presence.

"Hold on, brother! Hold on! You stay right here with us!" Earl and the other soldier cried out for a medic, though none were in view. As each second passed, Tom's grip weakened.

Earl wondered if any medics were still alive. After what seemed like an eternity, one finally arrived, and Earl pulled him to Tom. Earl tried to read the medic's face, to steal from it some of the confidence that was fleeing his own visage.

"Stay with us, Tom!" Earl cried again.

"Hold fast, brother," gritted Tom. The pain was obvious, but so were the courage, love, and gentleness that seemed so unfitting for such a gruesome scene. "I know where I'm going, and so do you. Run fast." He coughed again and grimaced in pain, and a small amount of blood came from his mouth. Earl held his hand tighter as tears flowed down from his eyes, not yet willing to grasp the fact that his brother's life was fading before him. "Tell Ann, and Ma and Dad and little Sis that I love them and will be waiting for them . . ." Tom then coughed again and slowly turned his head and looked to the skies. Despite the pain, a look of peace covered his face as he gazed skyward and then looked back at Earl. It was at that moment that he breathed his last.

"Tom!" Earl cried out. "Tom, come back! Tom!" He looked at the medic, who looked back at him and shook his head.

"I'm sorry friend. He's gone." And then the medic was up and attending to the next body.

Earl remained on his knees, motionless. He did not have the capacity to take in what just happened.

"Earl, we have to get out of here!" said Jimmy, who had been watching the whole time. It had all happened so fast, though to Earl it had seemed like a moment without time where nothing could be heard other than the heavy breathing of his brother. "Now!" Earl looked up at Jimmy, and saw the look of horror in his eyes. He released Tom's hand, and with tear-stained cheeks, he took off running, with Jimmy at his heels.

As fate would have it, Ruth was at the Timmings' house the evening when the news came to the family. They were all sitting around the dinner table when they heard the car pull into the driveway, from which two men in uniform emerged and walked towards the house. As each head turned to look out the living room window at the approaching men, silence engulfed the room. No words could describe the feelings that each person felt at that moment, or those that they were about to experience.

Richard opened the door, saying nothing. He knew what kind of news was almost surely about to be given to him. And to his inexpressible sorrow, he was correct.

Dear Ruth,

My desire now is to share with you of days that transpired with peace and relative calm and of my sweet thoughts of you and when we shall see each other again. However, I must share other news of the kind I hoped would not come to be. News you may have already received.

We came under heavy fire several days ago; many didn't make it—among them, my brother Tom. That I am writing of his death at this moment is something I still cannot grasp; seems like yesterday that we were wrestling out in the front yard or lying in our bunk beds at night back home, supposed to be sleeping but just talking about whatever until late. So many memories are bombarding me. I know the two of you bonded well also, and that my loss is your loss too. I am sorry to have to share this hurtful news with you. I pray I never have to write such words again.

I think back to the night I first met you, how he was standing there with me at the time and saw my eyes light up. He encouraged me immensely in my desire to get to know you and even gave me a nudge toward you that morning in church. I wanted to punch him for it, though looking back I see it was just fear and pride and am now thankful for that nudge. By the way, I was so nervous when I went up to talk to you, though I guess without fear there is no need for courage.

Just months ago we were training together for this place, talking about what we'd do when we returned home, how he hoped to ask Ann for her hand in marriage. Instead, I held his hand as he passed away from shrapnel wounds while lying on foreign soil far, far away from Cringle.

I can still recall the moment of his passing with such clarity. Intense sounds of gunfire and bombing were all around us, and then everything went silent. When I regained my senses, I heard someone shouting my name and telling me that my brother was hurt, so I ran over to where he was and saw him lying there on his back, badly wounded. Memories of us riding horses together and fishing and playing in the lake and river, of hunting together in the winter woods—they flashed through my mind as quickly as lightning.

In shock, I knelt down and held his hand, but he could barely speak. Then he was gone. Still under fire, I was forced to move on and had to let go of his hand that still barely clung to mine. "Goodbye, big brother," I whispered, tears falling like rain. I was unable to give him a fitting burial, yet I am confident, as I know you are too, that he passed on to a much better place. A place where he now dwells near a mighty river that runs with power and peace forevermore. Maybe there are even some lakes and streams there for him to fish in.

I miss him, Ruth. And I miss you. Your prayers comfort me. With you each day, no matter how far away,

Earl

Ruth wept. For the loss she felt herself, and for the loss she was sure was tearing at Earl's soul, she wept.

Everything Beautiful in Its Time

Dear Ruth,

As I write this to you, I am sitting on a white-sand beach leaning against a palm tree on some strangely named island in the Pacific. Base camp and all its unceasing activity is a short distance behind me, while before me, just a stone's throw away, the vast ocean stretches out as far as the eye can see. In the western horizon, which right now feels so unbelievably close, is a glorious sunset that rivals any we have seen together back in Mountain and Cringle. I say "rivals" for I believe the ones we've seen together in Wisconsin were, and always will be, the best. Nonetheless, I wish we could be enjoying this sight together, away from all of this.

As I look into this picture of beauty to the west, I am reminded of something you spoke while sitting together for the first time by the lake at my parents' house; of how God has placed eternity in our hearts and has made everything beautiful in its time. With the splendor of the evening sky that night, you could not have chosen more fitting words.

Everything beautiful in its time. The deeper meaning behind these words has always seemed beyond my reach, and with Tom's passing and this war raging on, they are especially difficult to acknowledge. I cannot conjure up the memory of his death without feeling an intense jab of pain, and a chill passes through my veins with the thought of never seeing him again this side of heaven, of never talking about life or being encouraged by him, of never getting to see him as a husband or playing with his children.

I must admit that, like Jacob of old, I have desired to wrestle with God when considering this reality; for allowing Tom to be taken so young. The anger sometimes swells within me.

And yet through tears, clenched teeth and fists, and cries into the night sky, my heart is healing, and a feeling of warmth that is beyond my ability to describe seems to prevent it from growing cold. And those words that were once beyond reach now bring to me a comfort that is new to me. For I cannot look at Tom's death, and all the death that surrounds me here, as being without some kind of greater plan or purpose that is far beyond the grasp of finite human minds. As we've talked about in the past, there is an evil that roams this world and wields great influence, yet it is also kept in check by goodness, which is the stronger force. And we're all caught up in between this mysterious battle.

I must also remember that death, which comes to all, no longer holds any true, lasting power for those who walk by faith but is rather a doorway into white, untainted shores that we were destined for.

Therefore I know, regardless of what my feelings would tempt me to believe, that everything is truly beautiful in its time, and that there is a season for all things. I know this, in part, because of the wondrous sight before me that exists simultaneously with all the brutality. I know that in some time long ago, likely in every generation that has come and gone, some young soldier like me has looked upon a similar scene of beauty and felt the same things I now do. Nothing is new under the sun, as we've been taught. Beauty, hope, brokenness, and suffering—they all exist together in some unfathomable way, even in Mountain and all of northern Wisconsin. It seems we just have to open our eyes and it is all there to see. Perhaps that is why some people don't open their eyes: fear of what they might see or find and the action steps that it calls them to.

And as we've been taught, all storms pass, and in time, can leave an indescribable beauty in their wake, both in the skies above and in the human heart.

I know what lies beyond the horizon too, behind the splendor of the setting sun and the veil of the darkness of war. A place that is set within the hearts of all who live and breathe. A place where no more tears or pain exist; a place that now draws my heart towards it more powerfully than ever before. And as it does so, it also draws me to you.

I love you, Ruth. I miss you dearly, as I do each day and each moment.

Earl
March '45

Earl sealed the letter and sat before the calm waters for a while longer. To his dismay, he knew this moment would soon pass out of sight, replaced by the storm clouds of the war. Slowly, yet with unyielding resolve, he rose and took the letter to the mail tent, then returned to his unit to make preparations for their departure.

Soon he would be fully engaged in battle once again, where the validity of all the words that he had just written would be tested in ways he never could have imagined.

Healing Rain

June 2, 1945
From Earl's journal

Our passage to the island on that early April morning faced considerably less resistance than the previous invasion, though once we landed on the shoreline and began pressing our way forward, the Japanese would make us pay dearly. With minds still fragile from previous battles, we would once again face unparalleled physical and mental duress.

And then it happened: an explosion with such force that it catapulted me backwards onto the sand, along with the feeling that something bit me in the shoulder. Shocked and dazed, I could hear voices of men crying out in agony in every direction. My vision and hearing began to slowly fade, and in a surreal sort of way I could feel my senses diminishing. In that moment, which I somehow remember clearly, I had a vivid flashback of Tom lying wounded and dying, though it passed quickly and was replaced by images of other men in my company lying wounded on the ashen ground.

And then I realized I was not imagining these images. One young man lay just feet from me, dead, his eyes open but not seeing.

Another son who would not be coming home.

And then everything began to quickly fade, and I was surrounded by blackness. Just then, as I was told later, two medics arrived and began working on me, reviving my consciousness. With rapid precision, they cleaned and wrapped my bleeding leg and shoulder as best they could, speaking in a commanding tone in an effort to keep me from slipping away like so many others did already that day.

I strayed in and out of consciousness while being carried on a stretcher through the shallow waters towards the landing craft that would transport me back out to the ship. Of this I remember only glimpses, faint images of the water lapping at their legs and a pain unlike any that I'd ever felt. Writhing in that pain, which was not yet as severe as it would be once the shock wore off, I could again see the flames and plumes of smoke rising from the island and the sounds of countless explosions. And at the same time, looking in the other direction, I could see the glimmering sunlight on the water in the distance and the endless ocean behind it. I don't know how this happened, given the circumstances, but the sight of such tranquility amidst destruction arrested me, and in the midst of what could very well have been my last moments on this beautiful world, I felt a sense of peace.

Soon I was lying on a cot that was fastened to the deck of an LST, which was pressed into hospital service due to the large number of casualties. So numerous were the wounded that there was no room for me below. Pain throbbed constantly beyond anything I had ever experienced. Many other men on the ship were injured more severely, some dying right before my eyes.

By this time I had grown more accustomed to seeing death, and though I was at the brink myself, I had not grown completely numb or desensitized to it like so many others. It seemed that for every life that I saw perish, whether American or Japanese, thoughts passed through my mind of their mothers, fathers, wives, and children back home who would mourn when hearing the news that their loved one would not be coming home. This fueled thoughts of Ruth and my own family, and strengthened my will to fight through this.

The ship departed that evening, and to the chagrin of its passengers, it passed through a heavy storm. Wind howled, thunder and lightning raged, and large swells smashed against it causing water to splash onto the deck. Every drop of saltwater that fell on my wounds, especially my leg, felt like tiny daggers being jabbed into me, over and over, and I writhed in agony so intensely that I loosened the straps that held me down and fell off the cot onto the deck, crying out in despair.

Then, intense rainfall poured down, stinging my wounds slightly, yet almost rinsing away the pain. Once, in between the rushes of pain, I pulled myself to my feet and dragged myself along the railing in an attempt to aid other hurting soldiers, though I was quickly escorted back to my cot like a child who had sneaked away from his bedroom at night. Disoriented, I really didn't know what I was doing. I just heard their cries and moans, and went to them.

It would be a journey of great pain.

Hours passed that seemed like an eternity, and the storm both in and around me raged on. The dressing on my wounds had to be changed several times, as the blankets they laid over me couldn't keep me dry for long. I don't know how those nurses found time to attend to me, for there were so many wounded, so much blood. Again I tried to leave my cot and come to the aid of other wounded soldiers, but this time my body, too broken and battered, simply would not allow it.

Eventually the storm began to subside and the waves calmed, leaving the water smooth and peaceful, the sound of the once violent wind now fading into a light, comforting breeze. Up above, dark clouds retreated and the stars began to emerge.

It was in that moment, when the first star became visible; when light finally overcame the darkness, that the harrowing pain in my leg and shoulder caused by the continuous onslaught of water and pounding waves, and the fatigue caused by my labors throughout the storm, finally took their toll on me. The last thing I remember was a deep moan and a desperate cry while clutching on to the silver locket Ruth had given me. Then I faded.

Earl awoke hours later to the sight of the sun gently rising over the water in the east. He stared at it from his cot, amazed by the stillness of the morning. For a moment he wondered if he had passed into the beyond, until he felt a growing pain rising up in his body that confirmed otherwise. He moved his fingers and toes, and to his relief found that he was still intact. Soon, however, after gazing into the sunrise like a child, he faded away again.

He woke again later, this time in a quiet, brightly lit room where other soldiers, many of whom were wrapped in white bandages, lay on beds all around him. A sense of fear instantly shot through him. He was unaware of where he was, what had brought him there, or what injury he had sustained. He could still feel the pain in his leg and shoulder in his body, though his senses were now so subdued that he barely noticed it. After a few moments, the fear dissipated as he felt comforted in some special way, perhaps because of the serenity of the place. He closed his eyes, savoring the feeling, and again passed into rest.

"Hi, Earl, can you hear me?" Earl heard the soft, comforting voice grow louder as light entered his mind. For a moment he wondered if it was Ruth, though as his disorientation lessened he knew that couldn't be. Nonetheless, the voice was as close to angelic as anything he had heard since he left the Midwest.

"Yes," he responded weakly. He cleared his throat and tried again. "Where am I?" he asked.

"You're in a safe place," she responded with a gentle smile. "It's early April, and you're at a US military hospital, far from the battlefield. We're going to take care of you now." As she spoke, two doctors came over, and with skeptical, astonished looks on their faces began to speak to him.

"Young man," one began, having to stop and search for the right words, then leaning over close to him and speaking quietly, "you are . . . you are fortunate to still have both legs on your body. This is one of those scenarios that we rarely encounter, and we stand here without much of an explanation."

The other doctor went on to explain that they had been expecting to amputate his entire right leg when learning of the nature of the wound. The medics who tended to him on the island likely cleaned and dressed his wounds properly, but the subsequent moisture and exposure to unsanitary ocean water would normally make things worse. However, the rainwater that pummeled him on the voyage and the multiple redressing of his wounds to keep him dry may have stopped the spread of infection and induced healing. But neither doctors were certain of this, and leaned in favor of it being a mystery. He would have to be monitored closely, and there was no guarantee that his leg would be restored to complete function, but there was hope.

Earl breathed in deeply, and a small smile came over his face despite the constant throbbing of pain.

"I'm not so sure it was just good fortune," he said in a weak but confident voice. The doctors smiled, not saying anything in response, but they took the young man's words to heart.

"And we probably don't need to tell you this," one of the doctors continued, "though due to the nature of this injury, together with the wound to your shoulder, you will not be returning to combat. As soon as it's time, we'll be sending you home." The doctor put one hand on Earl's good shoulder, then continued, "Thank you, Mr. Timmings, for your service and sacrifice."

Another groan came from Earl at the news, and he turned his head and looked solemnly out the window. He was sorrowful that he could not return to help his comrades, whom he had grown so close to. Yet he was relieved, as any man ought to be, that he would be returning to his home—and his loved ones. A tear slipped down his cheek, followed by another, each carrying a load of emotions.

After the doctors left, the nurse, who had been standing nearby, came over and sat next to him.

"I overheard your conversation. I'm guessing this is more than just good fortune too." Earl looked up at her and was again comforted by her countenance. Though he knew nothing about this young woman, she seemed like a sister and confidante to him at that moment.

Another month had passed by the time Earl boarded the ship, departing the Pacific theatre to return by water and rail to his homeland.

Now, sixty years later, Earl rose from his seat on the porch and walked to the edge to look up into the sky. He recalled with striking clarity his emotions while aboard the ship heading for home. Amidst all the swirling emotions, none was as powerful as his eagerness to see Ruth.

He reflected on the statistics of the war that he had learned in the days and years that followed: the horrific experiences some soldiers underwent in the field, in the Japanese prisoner of war camps, and those of the Jews in Hitler's concentration camps. These horrors all surpassed his own. There were the airmen who were shot down over the sea and spent weeks adrift at sea, along with navy men who floated helplessly in the cold waters after their ship was destroyed, being picked off by sharks that came in to feed. The immense loss of life on both sides was staggering—in the Battle of Okinawa alone, where Earl had been injured, Japan lost a hundred thousand soldiers; the Allies suffered more than sixty-five thousand casualties; and tens of thousands of civilians were killed, wounded, or committed suicide. Suicide that was in large part because of the Japanese soldiers' urging, convincing them that Allied soldiers were barbaric and would rape and pillage them in light of their victory.

And he thought about how it all finally ended after the big bombs were dropped on Hiroshima and Nagasaki. Bombs that would undeniably wreak their own havoc, but that some believed would also spare many lives by avoiding the planned ground invasion of the Japanese mainland.

One of his comrades-in-arms had told him about his brother, who was trained for tanks in the European front and who had crossed the Rhine River at Alms to engage in battle against Germany. Afterward, they were sent to Switzerland to prepare for a heavy ground invasion against the non-surrendering Japanese and were part of a large fleet of ships when they departed Europe. However, their ships soon turned around and headed back home to the States. The soldiers didn't know why they changed direction, but when they arrived back at New York Harbor, they found themselves in the middle of great celebration and learned of the Japanese surrender. Yet the soldiers' celebration was less ecstatic, mindful of all they had been through and seen, as well as the loss of life that Fat Man and Little Boy, the two atomic bombs, had caused. It was a difficult reality to grasp.

The memory of all this now rekindled old soul-wounds in Earl that he had suffered so long ago. Parts of his body still felt them too. Rarely were these reminders potent enough to knock him down, and never were they strong enough to keep him down, but they were a humbling reminder that some wounds, though able to be overcome, never completely go away.

Ride With Me

June 8, 1945
From Earl's journal

    That I'll be seeing Ruth tomorrow is something that I cannot fully grasp right now. It's hard to believe that it's been over two years since I have last looked upon her face or heard her voice.
    Thank you, God, for bringing me home.

Earl peered out the windows as the train neared the depot on a late Friday night. A strange, potent mixture of sorrow and elation ran through him as he sat there still as a statue. Above all, though, he was just grateful to be back in the Midwest.

He remembered the train ride over two years ago, when he and Tom had sat together on their journey west. He recalled Tom's words on holding fast while over there, and as he did so, a lump emerged in his throat. He had not yet been able to say a fitting goodbye to his big brother.

With a heavy heart he drew his gaze away from the window and picked up his bag, then walked towards the exit. The train was virtually empty and eerily quiet. He stepped off the platform and took in a big breath of air, then began looking around for his family. He didn't have to look long, however, for within seconds he heard his own name shouted from down the track. There, running toward him with a look of great anticipation on his face, was his father. Earl's heart was lifted high, and a wave of relief washed over him. They embraced, father holding son tight, tears streaming down both their faces.

"Welcome back, son," said Richard in a tender, choked-up voice, holding him. "We've missed you."

"I've missed you too," he said in a voiced muffled by his father's shoulder, "more than I can say."

After they released each other, Earl looked around for the rest of the family.

"Your mother and sister wanted to come with," said Richard, "but being so late, I convinced them to stay home and keep the house warm for your return. And Ruth—" Richard paused for a moment, delighted as Earl's eyes widened at the sound of her name, "—she was called away suddenly for a funeral of an old family friend, though they will be back tomorrow afternoon. She was just distraught over not being able to come, but we assured her that it was right for her to go."

"Thanks, Dad. After all that has happened, I suppose I can make it through one more day apart. And it'll be good to be rested before I see her." They picked up his bags and began walking towards the car. "I cannot wait to get home."

Though Earl was exhausted, he could feel the intense longing to see Ruth. In the weeks since he'd learned he was coming home, he had allowed himself to daydream about what it would be like to see her again after so much time apart. Just one day more, and the dream would come true.

He wondered if his father had intentionally come alone, for now it seemed best to have some one-on-one time together before reuniting with the rest of the family. Earl had so many questions about the family and hometown.

Nothing was said yet of the battlefield. Earl knew that his father's military service would allow him to relate to what he had experienced without any words being spoken.

For Richard, knowing what was going through his son's mind was enough to make his heart ache—for all the things Earl had gone through, especially the loss of Tom. He knew that there was so much more behind Earl's tired voice and weary eyes—so much pain, shock, and blood. For part of the drive, Earl dozed off, comforted by his father's presence and the sound of the tires humming on the road underneath, a road that would lead them home.

In his dreams, though, he had not yet fully left those Pacific islands, nor would he for some time.

They arrived home just after midnight. Patricia was standing in the living room looking out the front window when she saw the headlights. Her heart leaped as the first gleam of light broke through the trees and illuminated the driveway. For hours she had been in and out of short naps, getting up frequently to walk about the house, not knowing whether to laugh or cry, stealing numerous glances out the window and doing everything she could think of to make the house warm and welcome.

Her boy was coming home, and she could hardly believe it. Though the Timmings family suffered a great loss with the passing of Tom, it was not broken. And it was now regaining another piece. Joy and gratitude filled her heart.

Patricia rustled her sleepy daughter from the couch, as promised, and rushed to the door and stood on the porch. Though she tried to keep herself together, there was no holding back the tears.

Aroused from his deep dreams of squirrels and rabbits, Danny rose from his nap by the fireplace. He immediately sensed an excitement in the air, heard the car coming down the drive, and followed them outside. When the car came to a halt, and he saw Earl step out and heard his long-lost master's voice, Danny burst towards the car like a racehorse bolting out of the starting gate. Here was an energy the family had not seen since before Earl left. Earl knelt down as far as he could and gave his dog a big hug. Danny's body shook in excitement, and he emitted groans of overwhelming joy as his tail wagged like a flag in a thunderstorm.

Patricia began walking towards him, slowly at first, and gradually picking up speed. Earl stood up and went to her, embracing her with his good arm.

"Hello, Mother," he said in a gentle and weary voice, "I missed you."

"Welcome home, son. Oh, we missed you too! More than you'll ever know!" she said while sniffling. She had no more words to offer, only tears.

After a long embrace, Earl turned towards Stephanie and gave her a big hug as well. Tired and groggy as she was, her face radiated with happiness now that her big brother was home.

They went inside and sat around the table, reveling in the joy of reunion. In between the conversation were moments of silence that were neither long nor awkward but nourishing. Each sat under the peaceful, golden glow of the soft kitchen light, cups of coffee in their hands, with sounds of crickets and bullfrogs coming in through the windows.

And yet there was a solemn matter that was not far from any of them.

"Son, if you're not ready to talk about this, we understand. Though if you would like, we thought we'd take you up to see—to see Tom's grave on Sunday," his father said simply, running his fingers gently around the coffee cup while awaiting a response.

"Yes," Earl responded. "I would like very much to go up there. I haven't had a chance to say a real goodbye yet." He paused and looked out the window awhile before speaking again. "All I could see while looking out the windows of the train today was your faces, and Ruth's, and what I envision Tom's grave to look like."

When Earl went to bed that night, Danny waited eagerly at his bedside, wagging his tail, his eyes looking longingly at the empty spot on the bed where he used to lie. Earl smiled and let out a low laugh.

"Come, friend," he said, patting the mattress. Danny leaped onto the bed and curled up next to him, pressing his back into Earl's chest.

"Oh, this is good," said Earl.

With a soft, cool breeze coming through the window along with all the sounds of the night, Earl fell asleep after just a few moments of staring at the ceiling and out at the old, familiar sky. While the war still showed up frequently in his dreams, this night it did not. This night he was given sweet, lasting sleep of a kind previously unknown to him. It's possible that even his dreams were too tired and exhausted to show themselves, or that something much stronger was keeping them at bay.

Earl woke the next morning and for a moment was unable to discern if he was awake or dreaming. The comfort and familiarity was overwhelming; he could scarcely take it in. Aside from the short time at the military hospital, it was a great contrast to what he had been used to for so long. He looked over at the clock, which revealed that he had slept for nine hours—an almost unfathomable amount of time to him, for he had not slept this long in years.

Danny was still snuggled up next to him, his face just inches away and his endearing eyes looking deeply into his master's as his head lay on his chest. As soon as Earl shifted slightly and revealed that he was awake, Danny's tail began to flop up and down on the bed while the rest of his body was still as a statue.

Earl just lay there, motionless other than the short strokes of his hand over Danny's head. The sound of birds singing broke the pervading silence, and the fresh scent of late spring and the morning light poured through the window like grace from heaven. Feeling half drugged by the serenity of it all, he continued to lie there for a time, eyelids heavy, mind and body rested but still fatigued.

Earl was in no hurry to leave this setting. Yet the knowledge that he would be seeing Ruth that afternoon overpowered every urge to remain there. He was also powerless to overcome another more immediate draw: the aroma that rose from downstairs. The unmistakable smells of pancakes, maple syrup, eggs, bacon, sausage, and coffee all mixed together to form something that resembled bliss.

Slowly rising from the bed, his injured body still feeling stiff, Earl made his way downstairs, with Danny at his heels, and they were greeted warmly by the family. Since breakfast was still being prepared, Earl decided to go for a brief walk down to the lake with Danny, as they had done so many times in the past. Danny went out ahead to secure the trail while Earl gratefully absorbed all the familiar surroundings.

After sitting by the water for a short time, they returned and enjoyed a leisurely breakfast together, reveling in the taste of all the food that Patricia and Stephanie had prepared. They talked of just about everything, including Earl's plans for the day, and the feeling of sitting around sharing coffee and food was simply wonderful.

Despite all that was shared, Earl did leave one detail unspoken.

That afternoon, Earl and Danny climbed into the pickup and set out for his house in Cringle. He was so thankful to be able to own this place, and while overseas he vowed that if he were to return alive, he would pour his strength into restoring it. But now he was on a mission to retrieve an object from the house that stood for something of incalculable worth, something that has been on his mind ever since he left for the Pacific.

Though anxious beyond measure to get to Ruth's, he lingered awhile, walking around the property and envisioning what could be and what it would take to get there. *Soon this would be home*, he thought, and there was something about this reality that caused the flame in his heart to flicker wildly.

Just before leaving, Earl walked inside and lifted a loose plank of wood from the floor and retrieved a small box. He held it for a moment before putting it in his pocket.

But with this stirring of heart came an unbidden thought that was not new. It had revealed itself to him while standing atop the deck of the ship and while sitting quietly on the train on the way back to the Midwest: did he have what it takes to be Ruth's man? And how would she react to him after all he had been through? He was aware that though the war had not crushed his soul, it had bruised it, and he knew Ruth would be able to discern this immediately. His heart sank at the thought that it might be too bruised for her—or rather, more bruised than she deserved. Would the girl of his dreams still want to be with him?

He shuddered at these thoughts, and then the anguish turned to anger at the war, which had taken the lives of so many good men and left its permanent mark upon his body. Without knowing what he was doing, he wound back and punched the wall and drove his knuckles through the unpainted plaster.

He was on the verge of taking another swing when Danny yelped, and then rubbed his head against Earl's leg. And just as soon it had come upon him, the anger dissipated. He removed his white, dusty fist from the plaster, and though it was throbbing, he unclenched it and folded his hands together, and got down on his knees, where he stayed for a moment, praying for peace, grace, and strength. As he did so, he felt strangely lighter, as if a burden was being physically removed from his shoulders. Startled, he turned around, but the room was empty, save for Danny, who was looking at his master worriedly.

As the two of them drove off down the road, Earl felt a deep longing to drive by Tom's place. He stopped the truck on the road in front of the house and looked at it with heavy eyes.

"I miss you, brother," he spoke softly. Earl took a deep breath, overcome by the reality that now made this home vacant and quiet. Before his eyes flashed scenes of nieces and nephews running through the yard. Scenes that would never come to pass. More than once, he had to remind himself where Tom now was, and with that knowledge he slowly drove away.

In his heart he pondered his choices. He could choose to be thankful for the years that he had with such a wonderful brother, one who left such a strong legacy of integrity and generosity. Or he could go the way of anger and bitterness over what he no longer had. In his heart, he knew which choice was better, and in a manner of surrender he whispered the words, "I will go that way." He drove on, looking out into a far-stretching field that sat under open skies, admiring the beauty that passed by and soothed by the wind blowing in through the window.

Later that afternoon, Earl took a long nap that supplied him with additional energy and vigor. He arose with a tremendous sense of purpose, and after washing up, he again climbed in the truck with Danny and set out for Ruth's. More eager than he had ever been in all his life, he was convinced that the open road had never felt so good.

He could still hardly believe it; after all that he had been through, after wondering so many times if he'd ever make it home, and then wondering why he was among the few in his company who did make it home, he was now driving with his dog in his pickup truck, going to see his girl.

The drive to Ruth's seemed to pass by in a flash. He pulled into the Bensons' gravel driveway, and the house came into view. And there she stood, true as the morning sunrise, looking as gentle and beautiful as ever.

Ruth stepped forward and walked slowly to the edge of the steps with what Earl believed was a perfect, spellbinding blend of composure and anticipation. However, once he pulled the truck to a complete stop and he looked her in the eyes through the windshield, she quickly descended the steps and ran towards the truck.

Earl did his best to get out quickly and meet her halfway, but he barely had a chance to get both feet on the ground before she was in his arms. After some time spent searching each other's tear-filled eyes and smiling faces, Ruth buried her face in Earl's chest. Though the force of her embrace caused his injured shoulder and leg a fair amount of pain, he was so happy to be holding her that he barely noticed it.

"I've been waiting for you," she said, sobbing, her voice broken and muffled by Earl's chest.

For minutes that seemed like hours, they held each other next to Earl's truck, caught up in a space and time set apart from the world around them. There was no way to describe their feelings to one another, so they simply held each other in the midst of laughter and tears.

"Oh, Earl, your leg and shoulder!" said Ruth as she released her grip on him and looked over his bandaged body. "I must have been hurting you!"

"Perhaps just a little," Earl responded with a grin and a slight grimace. "But it's worth it to hold you."

"I hate seeing you hurt like this," she said while looking at his shoulder, and then down at his leg, "but I should be thankful you're standing here before me in one piece." Her eyes moved back up and met Earl's, which were as watery as her own. Simultaneously, they both gently began to wipe the tears from each other's face.

"Let's go to the house," Ruth said. "My parents are probably going crazy by now waiting to see and talk with you." And she was correct. Initially about to step out the front door to greet him, when they saw the two come together, Steven and Cynthia remained in the house to give privacy for the sweet reunion.

Though while waiting, Steven took his wife into his own arms and they both enjoyed a strong embrace themselves, each resting in the joy that was sure to be surging through the heart of their daughter now that Earl was safe at home. Knowing several families and spouses who were not granted the gift of seeing loved ones return, they counted their blessings over this occasion.

Earl and Ruth eventually went into the house and reunited with her parents. They shared a meal together and spent most of the time sitting out on the back porch, where Earl was further refreshed by the view of the pond and the barn beyond the field. Earl shared a few stories from his experiences, but for the most part he allowed the others to do most of the talking.

Steven and Cynthia, as well as Ruth, quickly noticed a change in Earl. Though he still possessed the personality that they had come to love, it was marked by a deeper seriousness and unassuming nature. And behind his eyes they too could see evidence of a long, painful journey that would leave him forever changed. Thankfully, however, it did not seem to have stolen his soul as it had for so many others.

As evening encroached, Earl found an opportune moment to be alone with Steven, at which time he inquired of him relating to a matter of the utmost importance. Without hesitation, and full of emotion, Steven showered his blessing upon Earl's request and gave him an uncharacteristically big, manly hug that nearly squished him. Like Ruth, Steven momentarily forgot that Earl resided in a wounded body and felt bad afterward for nearly making it worse. But again Earl was so overjoyed that he barely noticed the pain.

With no time to waste, Earl asked Ruth if she'd accompany him for a walk along the river. He said he was desperate to hear its sounds and to see a sunset with her.

"Well, I suppose you could talk me into it," she said with a grin.

They climbed into the truck, both dogs gleefully jumping into the back, and drove to one of their favorite stretches of the river. They slowly walked along the riverbank, Earl sharing stories as best he could from the past couple years and leaving out details that he felt best to keep unspoken. And there were many that he was not yet ready to recall himself. Ruth wisely refrained from pressing him for more details, despite her desire to know what Earl had been through. Between her own inner voice within telling her not to and the voices of others who had warned her against prying too much too quickly, she deemed it best to wait for him to open up about such things. Yet she made it clear that she was always ready to listen.

As they walked along the water's edge, Ruth sensed a shift in Earl's manner. He always carried with him a sense of energy and excitement, albeit concealed under his poised, steady personality, but she felt he had an added dose of it that night. He was using a few more words and hand motions than he normally did, and his eyes looked forward intently and possessed an extra spark that she noticed each time he turned to look at her. He also took several deep breaths—as if he were preparing to reveal something.

Her curiosity heightened, Ruth now spoke sparingly and listened attentively despite having much to share herself.

She was also a bit concerned, wondering if he had changed from the war; if something wasn't right with him. They continued to walk along, smiling and exchanging glances, both romanced by the lush sounds of the river and the warm, gentle breeze upon their skin and the golden glow that was cast upon the land by the setting sun.

Earl could not have been more grateful for the agreeable weather.

As they arrived at a small opening under the willow where they'd sat so many times before, Ruth was worried. Why was Early acting strangely? Had something changed? But her questions vanished when Earl stopped and turned towards Ruth, looking deeply into her eyes without saying a word.

Breathless, and feeling as if her entire life and the world around her had gone still like the sun and moon did in the time of Joshua, she watched as Earl slowly bent to one knee and carefully pulled a small box out of his pocket.

"Ruth," he said steadily, his heart pounding heavily in his chest, "many days I have wondered if I would ever be able to see your face again, and be able to say these words to you." He slowly opened the box to reveal a humble yet beautiful ring. "Will you marry me? Will you ride with me through all the days of our lives?"

Ruth felt her knees begin to give way, while an excitement burst forth from deep in her soul as tears streamed down her face. "Yes!" she cried softly, both her hands cupped around her face as she grasped what was happening. "Yes, Earl," she said, moved beyond words by the moment and the wonderful smile and tears that now fell from the man in front of her, "I will marry you!"

They returned to Ruth's that evening, smiles beaming from one ear to the other, and shared the news. Joy and celebration filled the house, as it did later when they made the announcement at Earl's. The great thunderstorms that had recently rolled through their lives had now passed and were replaced by springs of renewed hope and longings fulfilled that left them lying in their beds that night with hearts full and thankful. Though they were wise enough to know that life would hold more storms in the future, this was a time to be glad and enjoy what had been given them.

June 9, 1945
From Ruth's journal

> Earl, though wounded in both body and soul, has returned safely from the war. And with him came a ring that will soon symbolize the binding together of our lives. Words cannot describe how I feel right now, nor how wildly my heart was beating while watching him kneel to one knee while standing before me under the willow tree beside the river.

Ruth closed her journal and set it on the nightstand by her bed, then rose and walked to her window. There she stood staring wistfully into the night, basking in the breeze that lightly blew into the room and made the lace curtains sway ever so softly. The sky was full of stars and scattered, slowly moving clouds, and the sounds of crickets filled the air.

After a few moments, she looked intently towards her dresser, where a small letter sat upright with her name written on the front. Earl had given it to her just before he left for the night, asking her to wait until bedtime before reading it. She could wait no longer.

Dear Ruth,

> *If you are now reading this, it means that you have accepted my proposal to follow me through life. Together we shall traverse through good*

times and bad, through fishing, shopping (this will be among my greatest sacrifices as a man), reading, writing, riding through forests and valleys and fields, raising children (if the Lord wills it), stargazing and admiring fireflies, sitting in the canoe under the moon or before the sunrise, service and volunteering in all kinds of ways even when we don't feel like it, relational and day-to-day trials, some of which will be beyond our understanding or capacity to carry alone, and dogs and likely other animals that we will wish could live forever but will eventually break our hearts with their passing, and so much more.

And there is something I feel you should know. That ring that you now carry on your finger; that symbol of my love and affection for you, was not purchased recently. Rather, I obtained it just days before I received the letter that carried me off to the Pacific. Those few days of having that ring in my pocket were a small slice of heaven. The sky was so noticeably captivating, the air so richly scented with smells of the countryside, and I could see goodness in just about everything I set my eyes upon. For I was on the verge of proposing to a lovely, unselfish, vibrant, life-giving, servant-hearted, long-haired girl who made me so proud to stand next to and walk beside and row in a boat with her. A girl I could let my guard down around and be completely transparent with; who listened to my thoughts, fears, and hopes; who probed my heart, and whose heart I wanted to probe and guard and know more deeply myself. A girl who made me laugh, whose wit and intelligence and fiery spirit splashed me with life, yet who is steady and true, gentle and loving, imperfect and growing, broken and beautiful.

No one, save the store owner, who took an oath of silence, knew that I had bought this ring. I did talk with my parents and Tom and a couple other trusted people about the prospect of marriage someday, but I kept the timing to myself.

And then the induction letter came, and with it all my hopes and dreams that grew so fast were suddenly, mercilessly, sidelined. In that one moment, everything changed. I'd stare at that letter in my bedroom before going to bed or while walking around the yard of my soon-to-be house in the dead of winter, letter in one hand, ring in the other, with no words to express how I felt but rather groans that carried meanings only God could decipher.

I hid the ring in a safe place at my property in Cringle, and in my dresser at my folks' place was a small envelope with a letter inside containing directions for what to do with my few possessions—mainly the ring—in case I didn't return from the war. The words "If I Die" were written on the envelope, along with my signature and the signature of the mailman. Ronald's usually a tough-minded man, though he became choked up when reading those three words, so I placed my hand on his shoulder and assured him I'd do everything I could to return.

The days to come were filled with much darkness, and with every letter I received from you, hope was refreshed. And every time I finished reading one, I would close my eyes and imagine you sitting there in the other side of the boat, either looking at me with your striking blue eyes or staring off into the distance where a beautiful picture of nature or a scene from the past, present, or future had captured you. (I could never be sure which one it was, though I often wondered.) And with my eyes still closed, I would ask for a safe return home to see those eyes again.

And through a voyage of pain, God did allow me to return, with physical and emotional scars that are overpowered by hope and Providence and the promise of joy, so long as we keep our eyes fixed on the unseen that lies all around us and ahead.

I love you, Ruth, and I am both thrilled and honored to be able to walk through life with your hand in mine.

Yours,
Earl

Earl picked up Ruth the following morning and together they drove to church. There they were greeted warmly by their friends and neighbors, all of whom were grateful for Earl's return and ecstatic when discovering the news of their engagement.

They sat in a pew together, holding hands and both beaming. But they were also reverently conscious of the fact that there were families present whose sons did not come home, and never would again. Yet the peace and power of that which they came to worship that morning overpowered and comforted the immeasurable pain of loss, and a sweetness like the dew of spring hung in the air.

Later that day, as evening set in, they traveled to the cemetery near the church as planned. It was time for Earl to say goodbye. He slowly stepped out of the truck and walked to the small gravestone that was surrounded by fresh flowers. At the sight of Tom's name, inscribed in the black granite, he took a deep breath. He recalled Tom's having mentioned years ago at the dinner table that he'd want a very small stone for his funeral, and Earl was glad to think this one would have pleased him.

"So short, my brother—so short a life for you."

After standing there for a time, still as a statue, an eagle flew over and drew Earl's attention to the sky, where thick white clouds moved slowly across the blue canvas. The beauty and calm held Earl's gaze. In that moment, in a way that he struggled to later describe, he saw their past together flash through his memory, all the way up to their final moments together on the Pacific island and the day before when he drove away from Tom's old house. Then a gust of wind came through the forest on the border of the cemetery, causing Earl to look back down to the stone in front of him. It was then that he was forced to his knee from the weight of emotion, and with his head bowed low, he began to sob.

After holding it in for so long, he was now letting Tom go.

Ruth and his family stood back to give him space. She had been at the funeral for Tom while Earl was still in the Pacific and had shared in the pain of the Timmings' loss. Yet her heart ached all over again at the sight of Earl in this moment. Ruth had fought the desire to come to his side to comfort him, though after a time, she finally walked slowly up from behind and placed her arms around him. Silently, she shared in his grief.

June 10, 1945
From Earl's journal

So many memories and scenes passed through the eyes of my heart today while standing before Tom's grave, and with such speed and astounding clarity that I have never before experienced.

I saw the two of us sitting up later than we were supposed to as children, late into the night while talking about God, horses, hunting, and in later years, girls.

I recalled the battles we fought with each other while growing up, facing the questions that boys face as they seek to enter manhood, and how we grew so much closer and deeper as we grew older.

I remember well his finesse with the fly rod on the river and the holler he'd make when landing a big one; how he worked with me on my house in Cringle and was so excited for me and my future; how he encouraged me in younger years to just go for it in everything I did, and stood by my side through so much.

I saw him and Ann sitting around the fire and exchanging loving glances at one another, and hoping that I would one day have a relationship as pure and sweet as theirs.

I saw him gazing out the window on the train and looking at me with his encouraging smile as we headed west into the unknown.

I remembered his strength of character, and how nothing seemed to shake him even while he carried heavy burdens.

I saw the look of peace that came over his face in his final seconds while lying there on the island, holding his hand as he breathed his last.

I was, and always will be, blessed to have had him as a big brother.

Goodbye, Tom, and I look forward to reuniting with you when my time comes.

The Man by the Fire

Dear Ruth,

I'm not sure how to begin this letter. Something so strange happened on the way home last night. I suppose it had to be a dream, yet it felt so real, so alive. All I can do, it seems, is tell it like it is and hope you don't think I've lost my mind . . .

The days passed sweetly after the special homecoming weekend, one full of such powerful emotion: returning from the war and reuniting with family, asking the love of his life to be his wife, saying his final goodbye to his fallen brother, and beginning life anew. It was a time of picking up the pieces and assembling a frame for the puzzle of the rest of his life.

One week after his return, Harry, the local farrier and blacksmith, known far and wide for conjuring up interesting contraptions to aid in rural living, had created a special stirrup to better accommodate Earl's wounded leg in the saddle. Earl had wanted so badly to be able to take Ruth for a ride after proposing to her, a sort of commemorative ride, and Harry, upon discovering this, went to work with unparalleled fervency and determination.

"I'm going to get that boy and his girl out on a horse if it's the last thing I do down here in this old body," he said to himself deep in the midst of the creation phase.

Harry's words were as dependable as his anvil, and within a few days, Earl was again in the saddle. The Timmings family doctor was wary of his riding so soon, though knowing the animal's gentility and the rider's good sense, he was at least partly relieved from his burden of worry.

And so it was that Earl rode to Ruth's house for the first time in over two years, and led them on a slow sunset ride through the countryside, still careful to get Ruth home in time before dark set in. His leg became a little sore, though overall he was thrilled with how it held up, and it would continue to heal more and more with each passing day.

A week later, Earl and Ruth ventured out onto the trails again. It was another serene evening ride, just like the ones they enjoyed before the war, and all seemed to be perfect until Earl heard a series of gunshots in the distance. Before he knew what was happening, a series of unwanted memories, flashes of images and sounds, from the battlefield had sent his mind reeling. He was surprised at how much it affected him, for he had hunted small game a few times since returning and had experienced no issues when firing the shotgun. Frustrated, he slipped into a downcast demeanor, though he fought to hide it from Ruth so as to not ruin the mood of the evening.

As usual, though, it was no use. She could always see right through him, noticing even the slightest of changes.

"Earl, are you okay?" she asked gently as she rode up alongside him.

"Yes," he said in a resigned tone, "just a bit thrown off by those gunshots."

It was as Ruth had suspected.

They continued to ride along at a slow pace, side by side, and talked through what Earl was feeling. And for the first time since he returned, he shared a few details of what he experienced in combat. The memories were horrible, but he felt comforted by Ruth, who again did her best to simply listen and ask questions sparingly.

"Thank you, Ruth, for listening," said Earl in a tired voice.

"My ears are always open for you, Earl. We're in this together," she replied, looking straight into his eyes.

They rode on, both determined to enjoy the ride despite the setback. And they did.

As clouds gathered in the distance and daylight began to fade, they eventually turned back and made for home, arriving shortly before dark. Still feeling a bit rattled from the gunshots, and not wanting Ruth's parents to talk him out of riding home so late, Earl stayed just long enough to help Ruth unsaddle her horse before he departed. She tried talking him into staying, but he was bent on leaving. He assured her that everything would be okay, and then set out for the trail.

Halfway into the ride, the wind increased considerably. Earl knew that they'd be in for an unpleasant ride should the skies have decided to unleash the wrath that they were presently threatening. Soon the night became so dark that he could barely see Obie's head, let alone the trail in front of them. Second thoughts of leaving Ruth's began to swim in his mind, especially when considering the dangers that a forest carries after dark settles in.

"You are my eyes tonight, friend. Please get us home," he said while leaning forward, rubbing Obie's big neck to comfort him. Sometimes, though, a rider rubs his horse's neck to comfort himself as well. This was one of those times. Though Obie was a fine horse, he remained a flight animal, and there was no telling how he would respond to a flash of lightning striking close or a tree or branch falling nearby. Considering this, Earl held tightly to the reins with one hand and to Obie's mane with the other, leaning forward often and speaking in a steady tone in hopes of subduing the creature's mounting anxiety.

At a point in their journey, Earl had to choose between two trails: the longer one that would lead around the perimeter of the forest, or the shorter one that would cut right through it. While the shorter distance was tempting, the forest seemed foreboding to Earl given the hour and impending storm. And yet there was something inside him telling him to take the way of the forest. He could neither understand nor deny it.

"We have to risk this one, friend," he said, using his legs to steer Obie toward the forest. As raindrops began to fall, Obie let out a grunt in protest of the decision, though he obeyed nonetheless. They turned to the right and made for Sawyer Hills—the dense, rolling forest that sat between them and the safety of home.

They walked along at a brisk pace, both sets of ears attentive to all the sounds of the night. And then, just over halfway into the forest, Earl saw a small bright light in the distance, almost like that of a campfire. He was captivated, but his mind tried to resist acknowledging the sight, since he was unable to reconcile the existence of a fire in the middle of the woods on a night like this. As they walked on, though, the light was gradually becoming stronger, and there was now no denying its presence.

After a few more steps, Earl could see that the fire was off to the left of the main trail, perhaps fifty yards into the forest. Intent on getting home, Earl looked forward again and tried to refocus on the trail in front of him. But as he did, a strong gust of wind came hurtling at them, and at that moment he felt an overwhelming curiosity and compulsion to go to the fire.

Just then, a flash of lightning struck nearby that lit up the forest all around them, immediately followed by a crack of thunder so deafening that both horse and rider jerked. Then, another strong gust of wind swept through and caused a large branch to fall to the ground just feet away from the two. Obie was a disciplined, seasoned horse who could handle just about everything, but this was too much. He jerked backward, and Earl flew off and landed on the ground.

After a moment of lying on the ground, Earl slowly opened his eyes. After realizing what happened, he waited, expectantly, to feel a surging pain from his combat wounds. He began moving his fingers and toes—all good. He slowly sat up, feeling surprisingly fine other than a mild soreness. Obie was now standing above him, his head bent down toward his master as if trying to comfort and resurrect him.

"Oh, good friend, I'm glad you didn't run off on me," he said while reaching out to touch the big muzzle before him. "I think I'm going to make it."

Earl took hold of Obie's mane and pulled himself to his feet. He immediately noticed that the conditions had subsided considerably. Despite the rolls of thunder and quick flashes of lightning that still revealed themselves in the dark sky, an otherworldly peace and calm had engulfed them. The rain had ceased, and the wind, still formidable and making its presence known, was now less violent and threatening, as if it was commanded to respect and give heed to the travelers.

While surveying his situation, Earl again saw the fire. With a surreal state of mind that continued to battle his common sense, he took the bit out of Obie's mouth, both for his comfort and to prevent it from getting caught on a branch, and led them off the main trail in the direction of the flame.

As he drew near to the fire, he saw something that made him stop. There was a figure, unmoved, sitting alone.

"Come, join me," the figure said in a low, calm voice that penetrated the night and seemed to order the winds around it.

Earl's breath stopped. At that moment, as he would recall for all his years to come, he felt like both running away in great, unparalleled fear and also falling to his knees in awe over the sense of power and grandeur of the man. Never before had he heard such a voice.

The man's hood was pulled over his head, blocking the light of the fire from exposing his eyes. He had dark, shoulder-length hair, and high cheekbones with a strong jawline that was covered in stubble. There was something ominous about him—free and wild—yet somehow Earl sensed an air of gentility that made him feel no danger. Earl continued to walk closer, drawn on in spite of himself.

Earl tied Obie to a nearby tree and left plenty of slack so he could graze, pausing to marvel over how calm the creature was considering the circumstances. He walked slowly to the small fire, fueled by a half-dozen logs that burned steadily on top of a bed of bright, pulsating orange coals. The whole time he wrestled over whether this was really happening or was simply a delusion.

"Unusual evening for one to be riding through these woods," said the man as Earl approached.

"I know . . . probably not one of my better decisions," responded Earl. He wanted to add that it was an unusual evening for a man to be sitting alone by a fire in these woods on such an evening, but he kept quiet.

"You're wounded," continued the man, who watched as Earl had to sit slowly and methodically on the ground opposite of him.

"Yes," he responded after a moment, while leaning back against the trunk of a fallen tree, "and thankfully somehow no worse after that fall." Earl's voice trailed off when considering the implications. *How did I not get hurt any worse?* he wondered.

"Thankfully indeed," the man smiled as he spoke. "I could hear the thud of your body on the ground from here."

Earl nodded. The man shifted slightly to tend the fire with a stick, his eyes still veiled in shadow.

"Are you hungry?" the man asked.

Earl was suddenly aware of his growing appetite and somewhat surprised by it, for it was late and he had eaten a good dinner.

"Yes, I am," he said with a hint of caution.

With a smile, the man pointed towards the fire, where Earl noticed a small cast-iron pan with what appeared to be meat and fish on it.

"Walleye and venison from these lands," said the man. "I think you'll enjoy it. There is a plate and fork to your left." Earl could feel his mouth begin to water at the sight and smell of it, which had all of a sudden become rich and intoxicating. He reached over and took the plate and took a couple pieces from the pan.

"This is good," Earl said eagerly after he had taken a bite of both meats. "Real good." He had eaten meat of all kinds and was taught by his father how to prepare it well, though he couldn't deny that this might have been the best tasting he had ever had.

The man sat still, a slight smile still gleaming from under his hood while he stared into the fire, one leg outstretched and the other bent as he leaned against a small tree. Behind him, standing freely just a stone's throw away, was his horse—deep black with a long, flowing mane. Earl saw immediately that it was one of great stature.

After Earl finished eating, he leaned back slowly, still studying the man with fascinated yet wary eyes.

"You just returned from a war in which you suffered great pain and loss," the man paused, then continued, "and you're stepping deeper into a relationship—one that will test your manhood further," he paused again. "Do you think you have what it takes?"

Earl looked at him, amazed, trying to comprehend what he just heard and unable to begin to grasp what was happening. The storm, the fire, and this mysterious man who knew things about his life that a stranger simply couldn't. His mind kept telling him that he was dreaming, yet he was unable to deny the fact that it felt real as life itself. And in no dream had he ever tasted fish and meat so good.

"Do you think you have what it takes?" asked the man again, breaking in to Earl's introspection. This time, though, the man lifted his head and stared hard at Earl, and in doing so exposed his eyes that glimmered in the firelight. Earl was taken by them. Some kind of power radiated from within them, and for a moment he could have sworn he saw a red flicker in their depths.

"I believe I do," Earl responded with quiet confidence. If it were anyone else, Earl would probably have taken up defense and challenged the person as to why they were asking such questions, especially being a stranger. Yet with this man, he for some reason felt little need for defense but rather a raw comfort that allowed him to speak openly and with great respect.

"Good," said the man with gentle authority, slowly returning his gaze to the fire. "Because you do."

Earl looked up at him and then followed his stare back to the fire. His father had already spoken these words into his life, words of affirmation that confirmed his manhood. Though hearing it again from this man carried an extra charge.

As the night wore on, the man spoke of the future and themes that stoked a fire in Earl's heart: what it means to be a real husband, raising children, standing up for what is true and right no matter the cost, and living each day with the end in mind, and remembering that someone above and all around is always watching. He spoke of not getting too comfortable in life and of avoiding apathy, of sharing life with others, and of not fearing death while living, for in the case of Earl and those who follow in the same set of footsteps he does, this place is simply a portal to a home unlike any other. An eternal home he was destined for from the beginning.

"Who are you?" Earl finally asked after finding the courage to do so. His voice was full of both fear and exhilaration.

From under his hood, illuminated by the firelight, Earl could see a smile spread over the face of the man.

"You know me, Earl. You've known me for a very long time, though not as long as I've known you."

With those words, the man looked up at him with piercing eyes, and to Earl's great astonishment, they sparkled with unmistakable flames of fire. Earl gasped.

And not a second later, a bright white flash engulfed everything in his sight, including Earl himself.

Earl blinked a few times and tilted his head slightly in both directions. To his surprise, he discovered that he was lying on his back in the middle of the trail. Above him, visible through an opening in the canopy of trees, he could see the stars shining brightly just behind a line of passing storm clouds. Everything was so still, so silent.

Moments later, the silence was interrupted by the sounds of heavy breathing. He then felt something soft touch his face, then press firmly on his chest. It was Obie, gently nuzzling him in an effort to rouse his master.

"Well, hello there friend," he said in a groggy voice, smiling when hearing the creature respond with a low, joyful nicker. Earl slowly began to move all his fingers and toes, then his arms and legs, methodically examining his body to see if he sustained any serious injury, for to be lying on the ground as he was, he must have fallen off his horse.

Amazingly, he felt no pain, and was in awe that he did not aggravate his injuries. Slowly, he reached over and gently rubbed Obie's muzzle, then carefully took hold of his mane and lifted himself up off the ground, shaking his head. He could still feel the wind at his back, though it seemed to progressively subside, with faint thunder rolling in the distance.

After regaining most of his senses, a picture of the man by the fire entered his head. Though just as he was about to look into the woods to search for signs of a campfire, he all of a sudden heard familiar voices shouting his name in the distance and caught sight of flashlights that were drawing closer.

"Here! Over here!" he shouted as best he could, followed by a loud neigh from Obie who became aware of other horses. Seconds later, the sound of hooves hitting the ground grew in intensity, and three men rode up to him.

"Earl! Are you okay, son?" The voice was that of his father, and Earl could now recognize his face in the dim moonlight. Earl recalled few other times when he was so comforted to see his father.

"I am, somehow," he said with an exhausted but grateful voice. Two other men slipped quickly off their horses and came to his side as well—one of them Steven, Ruth's father. They asked questions about his physical and mental state and were relieved, as well as astounded, that he had not sustained further injuries from the fall.

And for reasons he was unsure of, Earl said nothing about the man by the fire.

Earl mounted Obie and rode home at a slow pace, encircled by the three men around him who were bent on ensuring his safe return. He was soothed by their company, and by the moonlight, scattered stars, and gentle wind. Yet he remained in a dreamlike mindset over what just transpired, or what he thought transpired, though his mind was too weary for deep pondering.

As they rode off towards home, though, he was again compelled to take one look back towards the woods where he thought the fire had been. But no fire could be seen. Though just as he was about to turn his gaze forward, he again saw a small but intensely bright white flash—so small but unmistakably real, breaking the darkness like a lone match in the dead of night. He stared in the direction a little longer, his weary eyes bent in thought, not ruling out anything, before returning his gaze to the trail ahead.

After arriving at home, Earl sat up and spoke with Ruth and a few others who had come to the house out of concern. He discovered that a large search party was being planned in the event that the men did not find him. It seemed to Earl that he had been gone for so long, though only a few hours had actually elapsed from the time he left Ruth's until now. The storm had moved quickly through the land.

Exhausted, he soon went to bed. Yet as he drifted off to sleep, alive and near was the memory of the man by the fire—his indomitable, enthralling presence; his words, though few, that seemed to defy gravity and cause the clock to cease ticking; and his deep, mysterious eyes that danced with flames and penetrated the deepest caverns of his soul.

The next morning, after some of the dust from the previous evening had settled, Earl sat down by the lake staring into the waters and reflecting on the words that the man had spoken. He knew, now more than ever, that deep wounds from the war existed within him, and the thought of carrying them unchecked into his marriage with the love of his life was simply unbearable.

In a strange way, though, he felt a lessening of some of the anger and bitterness that he had unknowingly been carrying around since his return. It was as if the fire from his encounter with the man had burned away the destructive emotions that were lurking in his soul, hidden from others, cleansing the filth and debris and leaving him refreshed and restored. Earl knew through the lives of others, and somewhat of his own, that soul restoration is a lifelong process, though he knew beyond reason that he had been touched in a special way by the experience.

As he sat pondering these things, the wind-borne ripples on the lake mingled with the sunlight and created a brilliant trail of sparkling bright white light that radiated upon on the water. It was a familiar sight, though on this occasion it was one that created in his thoughts a portal leading into another world—a heavenly place far beyond anything of this earth.

Earl grinned slightly at this, citing his active imagination as the source. Though deep within, he wondered. He believed that there was more to all the displays of light that existed on earth: sunsets, sunrises, moonlight, bright stars, fireflies, campfires, and all the other examples that evidenced the undying power of light and its dominance over darkness.

"There is more to this, friend," he said, gently rubbing Danny's head.

Later that evening, Earl shared the experience of the man by the fire and all the accompanying thoughts in greater depth with Ruth. She was the only person he told for some time.

Ruth looked at him with such a discerning look, one that silently communicated her belief that it might have been more than just a dream. In all their years together, it would remain something of which few words were spoken. Yet they would revel in the memory of it at times and keep it close to their hearts, usually late at night while lying in bed, when all the cares of the day yielded to deeper thoughts and considerations while the wind blew outside, and especially while eating fish and venison together at a campfire.

Under the Golden Maples

September 21, 2000—Flames before dawn
From Earl's journal

It is now early Sunday morning, and the sounds of a crackling fire fill this cabin. As I stare into the flames that light up this dark room, I am amazed that after building and enjoying thousands of these fires, whether inside or out, they still enliven my soul each time.

On this particular morning, I am reminded of that man by the fire, whose eyes still glow in my memory with a striking clarity.

After going for a walk with Jessie at dawn and enjoying coffee on the porch, the two of them climbed into the Jeep and drove off towards the church. Jessie waited in the vehicle while Earl was at the service, and afterward they walked around the cemetery. He spotted the gravestones of many who had once touched his life before he stopped at Tom's gravestone, where he paused for a long while, and then at his parents' gravestones.

And lastly, he walked to the maple grove and stood under the maple trees, aged but strong and vibrant as ever in color. It was at this very spot where he said his vows and slipped the wedding ring onto Ruth's finger so long ago. With a heavy but comforted heart, he sat down slowly and leaned his back against one of the trees, then pulled a small letter from his flannel pocket.

Dear Earl,

> *Tonight is the final night I will carry the last name of Benson. Tomorrow, I will walk with you down the aisle as a Timmings, and I am eagerly awaiting that moment. No other name could I carry so proudly, and I am as honored as any woman can be. I cannot wait to ride with you through this life together.*

Yours,
Ruth

"Honey, you look beautiful," Ruth's mother said to her as they stood before the mirror, making a few minor adjustments to her dress. Ruth's mother had sewn it herself, from a pattern Ruth picked out of a catalog. "I do believe Earl is going to simply melt at the first sight of you." Ruth gushed and laughed with delight, feeling her muscles relax as those words settled into her heart. More than anything, she hoped them to be true.

South of the Bensons' house, Earl and his father were doing what could be expected on such an important day: fishing. Richard felt it was appropriate to spend a commemorative hour on the river to revel in what was, what is, and what is to come, and he was able to convince both his wife and son, who met him with little resistance.

Just a week before, Richard had gathered together a group of trusted men—relatives and close friends, to speak words of wisdom into his son's life. The advice he received in that setting was invaluable; advice on marriage, faith, family, work, and what it really means to be a man. Now, as they waded through the waters only hours before the wedding, Richard reminded his son of these words and of the charge to press deeply into true manhood, for he was about to be entrusted with leading a wife—a great gift that would require everything he had to give, and then some.

As Earl listened attentively to his father, he silently wished Tom was with them sharing in the moment, and sadness flooded his heart. Though Earl reminded himself of where Tom was, and was determined to make good on the advice he received from these men, as well as the example that his big brother had made for him.

And so it was, hours later, that Earl was struck all over again by the sight of Ruth, veiled in white lace, walking toward him down the grassy aisle under a canopy of golden maples, her long auburn hair gently flowing behind her in the light breeze. Attendance was full on both sides of the aisle, everyone wearing their Sunday best and sitting on white wooden chairs. As Ruth passed, every single head turned to admire her beauty. All the while, a few large white clouds passed by slowly overhead in the deep blue skies. The poet in Earl was challenged to find words to capture the power in that moment, though his demeanor, smile, and tears spoke volumes—more than any combination of words could ever hope to.

However, he did manage to utter the words, "You are beautiful," in a soft whisper once Ruth stood before him, hand in hand while the sounds of a guitar and violin filled the air.

When the music stopped, the pastor began to speak. "The Book of Life tells us that there is a great mystery in our midst; namely, how a man and woman become one when they join together in marriage." His voice was loud and bright and projected over a few sparrows that were singing from the maple. "This oneness is symbolic of something far greater, something that came to be long before the dawn of time. But today, right now, we are going to talk of this union that holds great power and significance that is taken for granted by most. A union that can bring great joy and blessing to each other and all those who come into their path, given that each person embraces his and her responsibility in it.

"Earl, you are about to offer this woman a ring that symbolizes your love and dedication for her, and great accountability rests on you in doing so. You are called to love her as yourself, to serve and protect her, to be a leader in the home, to cherish and love her and to continually pursue her heart, to be willing to die for her. Earl Timmings, it is your lifelong endeavor to be the kind of man that makes it easy and desirable for Ruth to obey her Maker by following your lead as best she can, and to trust and respect you. Having known you all your life, I believe that you are up to the challenge and have considered the weight of it all, though in the presence of everyone here today, I must ask you: are you prepared to fulfill this task?"

"Yes, I am," Earl said steadily, recalling the man by the fire as he heard this charge.

"God bless you, young man," he said with a smile.

"Ruth," he continued, turning his attention to the bride, "as I look at the woman you are, and the kindness and virtue you exude, I am also confident that you grasp the weight of the relationship you are entering into, and your role as a wife to Earl. To come alongside him and support him, to respect him, to hear his heart and share yours, to continually grow as a woman and nurture your faith, gaining understanding and sensibility—which Earl, if he is wise, will depend upon greatly. In the presence of all here, do you embrace your task?"

"I do," she replied softly, her countenance steady as ever.

"And I now address this to both of you, Earl and Ruth: this union you are entering into today cannot be sustained to its fullness by your individual strength and effort. Rather, it will be by your reliance on God, who provides to all who reach out to him. Keep your eyes fixed on him, and fall to your knees often to cry out to him. And be thankful. Remember that the devotion and passion you share for one another will be in direct proportion to the hunger and passion you have for the one who provided you with this gift. He is your strength, your hope, your reason for living, and always will be. Keep that in mind when the storms come. And they will come. And they will pass."

The pastor spoke a few more words about marriage and challenged those in attendance that they, too, were a part of this joining and would be called upon to help nurture the union in the years to come. And finally, the words that Earl and Ruth had dreamed of hearing for so long were spoken: "I now pronounce you man and wife. Earl, you may kiss your bride."

Earl and Ruth looked at one another eagerly, and then Earl gently placed one hand behind Ruth's neck and the other hand on her back, and gently pulled her in and kissed her for the very first time.

"Ladies and gentleman, boys and girls, I now present to you Mr. and Mrs. Earl Timmings." A loud cheer went up into the air and was followed by a night of celebration and dancing that sent a buzz sweeping throughout the small town, and likely into nearby counties.

Later that evening, Earl and Ruth returned to the house in Cringle to spend their first night together in their new home before leaving for their honeymoon. It still needed some work, though it had running water, a fireplace, hardwood floors and a wonderful view of the sky from the porch, and neither Earl nor Ruth could imagine spending their first night together anywhere else.

And the moments were few in which they were not in each other's arms.

Early the next morning, they raced off to their honeymoon in the pickup truck that Earl and his dad had spent hours on cleaning and tuning up. The first part of their adventure would be spent at a rustic, cozy cabin on a big, beautiful lake in northwest Wisconsin. Then off they would go to the north shore of Lake Superior, where another, more luxurious, cabin would be their dwelling for the greater portion of their time.

The days ahead would prove blissful, filled with horseback riding, fishing, and sailing, the only sense of time coming via the rising and setting of the sun, both of which they could view brilliantly from the porch that wrapped around the cabin. They read books together while sitting lakeside or on the porch, occasionally driving to a nearby small town to visit quaint shops where Earl treated his new bride to a few special gifts and some ice cream. A couple times they rode bikes through country roads canopied by vibrant red, orange, and yellow autumn leaves, all the while in no particular rush to get anywhere.

One evening they ventured to a nice restaurant in a nearby town that bustled in the summer months, where they enjoyed a fine meal and glass of wine, followed by an evening of live music. That night, they fulfilled their longstanding love for dancing by doing so until they could barely stand.

The next day, they hiked the shoreline of Lake Superior and spent the night camping in a tent on a high ridge. Below, they could hear the waves lapping against the shore below, and above them the stars glistened brightly. They even witnessed the dancing northern lights, an unexpected sight that made them feel closer to heaven.

Late that night, sitting beside the fire in her husband's arms, Ruth just stared out into all that was. Earl watched as her eyes grew heavy and then closed after she could no longer fight sleep. Once she was asleep, he sat there motionless, experiencing an immense fullness of soul as the stars shone, the fire crackled softly, and his bride lay asleep in his arms. Soon he would have to wake her and go into the tent, though he treasured the moment. It was a gift, and he bade it to stay as long as possible.

Yet all things come to an end, as did the moment on the high ridge and soon their stay on the northern shores of the great lake. Though they were sad to depart, the excitement to return home and begin their new life together trumped all other emotions.

That Sunday night—the final night of their honeymoon and the night before Earl was to go to work in the morning and Ruth was to begin making preparations for her nursing classes, they sat together on the backyard porch of their home as twilight settled in. At one point they looked over at each other, smiled, and exchanged a few simple words that would be etched in their memories for all their days to come.

"So it begins . . ." Ruth said.

"Yes, so it begins," Earl replied in a low, confident voice. Then he grinned. "And I'm thrilled for the ride to come."

And so began their life as one.

Years So Full and Fleeting

Almost sixty years later, Earl now sat on the porch of their cabin. He had just returned from the church, where he had walked among the autumn trees and the cemetery, where the epitaphs that he had seen so many times over the years once again reminded him both of the brevity and value of life and relationships.

After a time, he pulled out a photo from the shoebox of him and Ruth standing before Lake Superior on their honeymoon. He smiled at the sight of it.

"If only time could stand still," he thought, cherishing the memory in his heart.

And then he looked up at the gently swaying treetops and the soft white clouds passing through the sky and was struck by the realization that so many wonderful experiences came to pass between him and Ruth because time did not stand still.

He reached into the shoebox again to pull out another letter. Only a handful now remained. As he reached in, he took a closer look at his hands and the skin that covered them.

"I'm getting old, Jessie. These hands are a bit of evidence."

Earlier that day, he had read numerous short letters and journal entries that were written in the decades following their marriage. Though now, with the letter he held in his hand, he was about to light a lamp over the final years, years that were perhaps the most emotional, deep, and wide years of them all.

And perhaps the most painful.

Dear Ruth,

We are told to number our days so that our hearts may grow wise, and that we may make the best of the opportunities presented to us. As we discovered, this was no easy task, as from time to time we wrestled with whether we were doing the best with the time gifted to us. Questions of all sorts—about how we're raising our kids, nurturing our marriage and friendships, serving our church and community, following hard after God—these ran through our minds more than we liked to admit.

Though in retrospect, I believe that we have done well with the time we were given, and that we have been a fine team in this life.

And as I look back over those years—those fifty amazing years that began one sweet, fine day under those golden maples, there is so much to remember. So much that I feel that trying to capture even a slice of it on paper is an injustice to the depth and beauty of it all. Yet I must try nonetheless.

I remember our first house, lying out on the porch and watching the stars together that night after our honeymoon. Laughing, crying, sometimes not saying a word, and all caught up in the moment and lost in the beauty around us, dreams of the future flowing like torrents through our minds. In the years to come, this stargazing while lying side by side, sometimes wrapped in each other's arms, would happen countless times.

Your first pregnancy came shortly after, and a thousand dreams and hopes that accompanied it were dashed by a miscarriage that tore at our souls and tried covering our marriage with gloom and despair. It was successful, but only for a time, as our eyes and hearts would again be opened. Soon after, another child was formed in your womb and would go on to see the light of day, and then a few more, each bringing incomprehensible joy to us both.

The way in which time began to move at lightning speed after becoming parents struck us both. Years filled with ups and downs, laughter and tears, and various stages that came and went so quickly and provided no owner's manual or checklist to follow. It seems, in retrospect, that in a blink we went from changing diapers to watching them walk down the aisle in their weddings and eventually have children of their own. Life does have a way of circling back, as we discovered with all those times they called us, sometimes late at night, asking for advice.

And through it all, I marveled at how you grew into such a wonderful wife, mother, and woman with each passing year. Your honor became the deepest of wells, and your beauty intensified with age.

Thank you, Ruth, for the gift of fatherhood, and for providing me with the privilege of being a grandpa. It's hard to believe our grandchildren are married, and that we have great-grandchildren—wonderful, highly animated and infinitely curious little creatures that showed us yet another season in this journey and brought new life to the family. I often shake my head when considering the breadth of our family, and I sometimes wonder why we were so blessed. Yet I know that this question has limited value, and that I should simply accept the gift and be thankful.

Earl paused for a moment and set the letter down on his lap. As he read that last paragraph, memories of sitting in the fishing boat or standing in the river with his grandchildren flashed through his mind.

He remembered the time when he and one of the grandsons were in the boat together, long after dark, a half-moon shining above them with stars glimmering all around, even off the water. They sat and talked of this and that, their fishing poles in hand. They had a good night of fishing too, with a catch every now and then that boosted their adrenaline and left them satisfied as they returned to their seats.

Eventually, just like Earl had done with his dad growing up, and then with his own children afterward, they all lay down in the boat a few feet apart with Earl's dog in between them, and covered themselves with a sleeping bag and fell asleep under the stars to the sounds of the night all around. Dawn would awaken them, and they'd resume fishing while brewing a pot of coffee, using a Sterno can to heat it and chewing on venison jerky, fruit, and a couple donuts. Before morning faded into afternoon, they'd return home, physically tired but with refreshed spirits.

Earl could feel his soul alight at the memories, and he smiled despite what he knew he was about to read. Resolute, he picked up the letter again and continued the journey.

Yet there were the hardships too—losses and great trials, some that we could not have imagined.
. . . Danny's passing, and the sadness we felt afterward. He was such good boy, my loyal

friend and shield-bearer against loneliness before you came into the scene. He continued to show his ardent devotion to both of us after, and my heart still aches at the thought of him now, so many years later. His light brown eyes always pierced us with such tender love and affection that we knew God delighted in these creatures that often outperform humans in certain areas, especially forgiveness. Creatures that, to our regret, live such short lives.

From the earliest days of our courtship until his last breath, taken while wrapped in my arms at the vet, I was so thankful that you adored him as you did. I can still see you standing by the kitchen sink later that evening after we buried him, looking out into the setting sun and beginning to cry.

As always, the pain would subside, and the years to come would bring a few more wonderful dogs and horses into our lives to enrich our days for a time before leaving us, breaking our hearts all over again. You know the names. At times we were tempted to close and seal our hearts to other animals, though we knew this was only an easy way out of facing pain and one that could lead to the hardening of the heart.

And we cannot forget a couple of those gregarious, sweet-tempered pigs. I never knew those snorting, messy animals could be so kind and personable. Bacon just never tasted the same after that.

. . . Of course, the loss of each of these animals pales in comparison to losing a child. Our Jill passed long before it was her time. Just like Tom. It is often said that one of the hardest things to bear is seeing one of your children pass, and this proved true. We pleaded with God for her life, which had not yet spanned thirty years, though it seemed he had other plans. Powerless to do

anything, I wanted so badly to wrestle with him for not bringing her back to us. I keep the words few on this, as we both know the depths of pain and desperation that we experienced.

I so look forward to seeing her again one day, as I know you do also. And as I sit here now, I can now find comfort in knowing that she is in a place of unbridled freedom, in the presence of the One who both gives and takes away.

. . . The challenges that faced our marriage. We knew they would come, though foreknowledge only girds one for a battle that they must traverse through. We were a bit shaken by the seasons where we just could not seem to connect like we ought to, challenged to find quality time with each other, learning how to grow and change together and afford grace to one another for our imperfections and failings. We clashed at times on how to raise our children and were forced to learn compromise and effective communication on a far deeper scale, as so much depended on our ability to do life together. It was sink or swim, and I'm so thankful that we kept pressing through the breakers.

Though through it all, we were able to experience the mystery of marriage; the bonding of a man and woman that runs so deep and wide and that represents something far greater, like that of a refining fire.

. . . The passing of our parents, who lived exceptionally long lives, and the slow, gradual healing that would follow. Even though we knew the hour of their departure was close at hand, and that green, unfading pastures lie in wait for them, the moment when the goodbye became real and final was so difficult to embrace.

Yet their memories would grow into such a treasure, the pain subsiding and replaced with the treasure of a lasting legacy. I still miss them dearly as I write this letter to you, and would love to be sitting around the dinner table drinking coffee and laughing under the soft glow of the overhanging lamplight, fishing with Dad out on the river as the sound of rushing water filled our souls with great peace and vigor, or enjoying a meal with your parents out on the back porch, reminiscing of the past and plotting the future while doing our best to enjoy the day at hand.

In some ways, I am haunted by the memories, as I know you are too. Perhaps now more than ever, I can still hear the sounds of the river as Dad cast his bait with a steady face and slight smile, and see Mother by the counter examining a recipe, all their imperfections washed away and replaced by their finer qualities, and my only comfort now is the knowledge that I will see them again one day soon.

Perhaps all of them—Jill, Tom, our parents, and Danny—will be waiting at the table for us when we arrive, coffee in hand, with laughter, tears, and overwhelming joy filling the room.

Though these were all deep losses, they hurt so badly simply because they were invaluable gifts to us. As we often said, the value of life is truly revealed and laid bare when it is threatened or being taken away. Thankfully, after the dust settled, these losses emerged and budded into deep-seeded memories that would strengthen the flame in our hearts long after the shedding of tears had passed.

I remember sharing with you of how I walked out on the dock one cold winter's night, overwhelmed with all these memories, along with the feeling that life was moving way too fast and not having enough arms to do all that I felt was before me. At my wits' end, I cried out into the moonlit sky, the frozen, snow-covered lake glowing with such radiant white light, the stars above in the deep blue sky twinkling and so still, so steady. I then went down to my knees and just looked up, and a great anger and frustration raged within me for a moment and then began to subside, awe and surrender taking over.

That night certainly wasn't the only time I reached that point of mental, spiritual, and physical exhaustion, though there was something about it, something powerful that caused it to linger in memory's vault. As usual, you just looked at me and listened, comforting me with your soft spirit and offering few words that carried such great weight in my soul.

Thankfully, these challenges and hardships grew us closer together and strengthened our bond over time, and as always, the storms would eventually pass and leave us to again enjoy the little things in life.

. . . The smell of spring, the splashing of water on our faces in the summer, the colorful morning walks down the trail in the fall, and the warming of our bodies in front of the fire after spending time outside in the biting chill of winter.

. . . Delving into soul-stirring poetry and stories and reading to one another, our minds and hearts fully engaged. It seems, in retrospect, that I did most of the reading, though I'm not complaining. Deep and wide was the satisfaction I derived from having you next to me while exploring all those pages, with stories, both fiction and nonfiction (though we know a good deal of fiction isn't really fiction at all) coming to life.

. . . Horseback rides of various speeds throughout every season of the year, every year. How blessed we were to have such an option! And as I reflect on it now, I find it remarkable that we were never seriously injured by those big brutes in light of all the rides we went on.

However, that time that a couple of grouse flew up and spooked the horses, sending you flying off the saddle into the brush, was a close call. I went from being terrified for your well-being to laughing uncontrollably after seeing you pop up from the brush, wild-eyed and smiling from ear to ear, your hat bent sideways and leaves hanging from your hair, a little dirt on your cheeks and chin. You normally held on to agitated horses as well as anyone, but that moment caught you at just the right time. Poor Silas! Unlike most horses who couldn't care less, I believe he felt bad for sending you flying through the air like a salmon at a fish market.

. . . Our visit to Peleliu in the Pacific where Tom died; Pavavu, the base island where I wrote you a letter while sitting before a beautiful sunset shortly before I was injured; Okinawa, the island where I almost died. I thought it might be traumatic, going back to these places, and while it was painful, your presence was a balm to my soul and a reminder of how blessed I have been. The feeling of you leaning against me, looking into that same setting sun, was beyond words. We then visited the cemeteries in the states where the fallen lie, so many young men. As mentioned, I believe we lived as full a life as we possibly could, though that trip was yet another powerful reminder that death is the destiny of every living thing, and how important it was for us to remember this in order to truly live out our days, no matter how many remained.

. . . Celebrating some of our anniversaries by returning to the cottage on Lake Superior where we spent part of our honeymoon. We also used that cottage a few times for family vacations, having to pack six suitcases in the car versus two. But what a treat it was for the both of us to be able to share such a special place with the kids.

And I have to admit, one of my favorite memories from those trips was the time we went out and bought you a new fishing pole, and how, on the first cast you took with it, it jammed on you and went flying out of your hands into the deep abyss and evoked a scream. Though I meant no disrespect, I lost control and began laughing so hard that I dropped my own pole in the water and nearly lost it as well. I laughed for a long time, as I'm sure you remember, partly because of how hard the kids were laughing. Seeing a tear in your eye and a sad look come over your face calmed my laughter, however, and my journey to the front of the boat to console you ended with you cleverly pushing me into the lake. Coming up from the water was refreshing, though, and the sounds of you and the children laughing and the dog barking made me grateful to be a dad that day. Not to mention a bit more wary of your intentions going forward.

. . . The times spent with the Jamison family and all those peanut butter and jelly sandwiches made for Beau and his siblings at the cabin, along with the fresh fish you often prepared for us. That family captured our hearts from the beginning, and I can still remember clearly the first day we met them at the church—how lost and anxious they looked when visiting for the first time, and how quickly they took to us after we opened our hearts and home to them. Time would bring a drift, and they have found their way back to troubled waters, though we continue to pray for them with unyielding hope.

. . . Our trips to Chicago and all those nights of dancing and walking along the shores of Lake Michigan, where vast and beautiful skies and water sat on one side while the bright lights of the city shone on the other. Though we truly enjoyed the city, and could have even

lived there, we did enjoy getting back in the vehicle and returning to our country home. I think we learned, at least to some degree, that a satisfying home is dictated less by whether it's city or country or somewhere in between but more so by the roots established, bonds created, and lives impacted by one's active, enduring presence in that place. And we also learned the danger of growing too attached to a home, for we know that our real home is still awaiting us—a home that will not require so many trips to the local supply store, if any. I just hope there are fireplaces and dogs there.

. . . And so much more.

Happy anniversary, Ruth. I love you, more now than ever, and deeper than I ever thought possible. And I remain among the most honored men that I should have the privilege to call you my wife.

Yours,
Earl

Sunset Ride

"Will you ride with me?" Earl asked his beloved while seated on his horse.

"Yes," she responded with a deep smile, her eyes still moist from the letter Earl had written her for their anniversary. "I would love to."

It was early evening, and they had just arrived at the Harmons' stables that were still going strong generations later. They saddled up and mounted the horses on their own, no small feat given their age. The horses were two of the gentlest, time-tested creatures in the herd; regardless, their children, who came to spend the day with them for their anniversary, came along just in case assistance was needed. Two of their sons, David and Seth, also decided to wait on the porch for their return. Earl consented to this, aware that anything is possible with these animals, and checked his radio to make sure it was fully charged and functioning properly.

With the sun moving closer to the west, they set out for yet another sunset ride.

"Those two just keep on going," said their eldest son, David, while watching them disappear into the forest.

"And they will until their final breath," said Seth, a wistful smile spread across his face.

The ride was breathtaking, with sunlight bursting through openings in the trees just like it did countless times before. They talked of how they wished these horses could run free, unfettered by bridle and bit and the weight and demands of life.

"I agree, honey," said Earl, "but they still manage to take pride in their jobs and love rolling in the dirt. So it must not be all that bad."

"No, I suppose not," said Ruth laughing. "And they get to carry us around. What could be better?"

"Ha! I can't conceive anything being better than that. Especially considering all the apples and treats we feed them."

They rode on gingerly, passing by patches of blueberries and crossing through small streams, and even saw a doe and two fawns pass over the trail in front of them. Deer, unlike many other creatures, never made the horses even a bit skittish. Ruth especially adored these animals, with all their gentility and gracefulness, and though she was not against hunting and enjoyed venison, she wished there was some way they did not have to be constantly hunted in life by man and beast.

Through deep woods, forest glens, and wide-open spaces they continued to ride. With no one his senior to exhort him for being out too late, Earl pushed the clock as far as he could. Yet night waits for no one and an end had to come nonetheless, though it came all too soon for the two riders. To the relief of their sons who were still waiting for them, they came riding slowly back to the stables at dusk, relieved smiles on both their faces illuminated by the lamplit porch.

From there, they all walked back to the Harmons' yard and enjoyed a surprise celebration with friends and loved ones. Tents had been set up and tables were filled with food of all sorts, and a big campfire burned steadily. The weather could not have been any kinder. A few clouds hung in the autumn sky, accentuating the stars that had begun to emerge, and a soft, mild breeze moved through the land.

Near the end of the celebration, Earl looked over at Ruth, who was surrounded by grandchildren and friends and wore a look of pure joy on her face. He just stood there contently, enjoying the sight of her being so filled, so alive.

After the celebration had ended, Earl and Ruth climbed into their truck and drove home together. They held hands the entire way, laughing and talking with full, thankful hearts. And once again, Earl intentionally drove slowly so as to enjoy every possible minute with his beloved.

A Flower Fading

February 16, 1996
From Earl's journal

Today was Ruth's birthday. It was another special day with the family, and once again Ruth found herself surrounded by a sea of grandchildren clamoring for her affection. And as usual, a warm smile beamed from her face the whole time that, I believe, warmed the hearts of everyone present. Mine included.

A few moments after seeing that smile, however, I noticed her wince and rub her forehead, while a look of mild confusion spread over her face. My heart sank. She recomposed herself quickly to avoid causing a scene or startling the young ones, though despite her best efforts to conceal, a few people noticed it. No one more than myself.

The silent nemesis cannot hide from me. Nor does it try to.

February 19, 1996
From Ruth's journal

> Oh God, I choose life. I wish to live; to enjoy more years with my husband and the rest of my family. There is no illness or infirmity that you cannot heal and wash away. And yet I know you work in mysterious ways and call people home when you choose, and if these are to be my final days, please strengthen my spirit and help me to finish well.

As Earl sat on the porch, he reflected that he had entered the new millennium without Ruth by his side. Several years had passed since he first learned of his wife's illness. They had sat together hand in hand at the hospital, where they heard their physician, his voice pained, speak the words, "Ruth, you are ill." Earl, now many years later, could still hear the doctor's words so vividly—as vividly as he could hear the sounds of Ruth crying in his arms later that evening while sitting on the porch under the starry skies. The same porch, and in the same spot, where he now sat with Jessie.

Yet those cries of Ruth's were not for a fear of dying, though death and whatever measure of pain it may entail was not something she eagerly awaited. The real source of the pain was the thought of having to leave behind her dear husband, children, and grandchildren and to not be able to care for them, to be there for the milestones of their lives. She knew one's passing can leave behind a great, influential legacy, and that God could achieve his ends without her. Nonetheless, the thought of leaving soon was a heavy burden to bear that night.

Haunted by the memory, Earl stood and walked to the railing and leaned against it while feeling the full weight of the shoebox memories that were about to come alive again.

"It is a somewhat rare form of brain cancer. Slow-moving but unrelenting and, from our vantage point, inoperable," said their doctor. Their grips tightened around each other's hand. Earl felt a surge of anger and powerlessness, with no physical enemy to assail for hurting his wife, the only thing assuaging his fury were the silent prayers said over and over in the recesses of his mind. Ruth was obviously shaken as well, though like her husband, her faith held her together.

The first time Earl noticed a symptom when looking at her, time stood still. His eyes froze on her as countless thoughts rushed through his mind. As much as he had always been mindful of the physical and mental ailments inherent with old age, there was no way for him to prepare for a loved one, let alone Ruth, having to face something that could possibly take her life.

As time progressed, Ruth's discomfort and confusion became worse, and Earl never could have imagined that he'd experience the agony of seeing his wife groan in pain and be able to do nothing about it, especially after all these years of being blessed with good health. She would frequently have headaches, sometimes minor, other times debilitating, which would force her down onto the bed, where Earl would be at her side with a cold washcloth on her forehead while gently massaging her arms and neck. It was a long, painful season of life that made him shudder even now, years later.

Thankfully, Earl and Ruth were able to work with their medical team to better manage her symptoms and bring a touch of relief. The disease itself did not retreat and much uncertainty remained, though Ruth was able to live relatively peaceably in the days that followed.

And what rich, unexpectedly fulfilling days they were. Each one was held onto as a lost treasure now found, with stubborn hope that one more, and more after, would remain. They enjoyed wonderful times together, strangely deep and poignant even though they were often spent right in or near Northwoods Memorial Hospital. Sometimes their conversations led them into laughter or tears, and other times they were more lighthearted, though those usually led to laughter as well. More so than ever in the past, these conversations held long pauses in between, where the two of them would just stare at each other or out the window into the skies, silently wondering if these were the final days, and if so, how many more of them remained.

Oftentimes their children and grandchildren would come to visit, and though they were heavy-hearted at the sight of their withering mother and grandmother, they were always encouraged by her warmth and ever-present glow and hope that lifted their hearts. The hospital was a pleasant one to begin with, with exceptionally compassionate staff and leadership, though the radiance that swooned from Ruth's room, especially when multiple members of the family were present, did not go unnoticed. Her children often came with hopes of bringing comfort, yet they were the ones comforted when leaving.

And leaving was always hard.

Days would pass when the nurses would smile at the sight of Earl wheeling his lady through the hospital, often stopping by the rooms of other patients where they would linger and ward off their loneliness, especially those who had little or no visits from family or loved ones.

As often as possible, Earl would get Ruth out of the hospital and stroll about in the country air, allowing her to enjoy the feeling of the wind on her face and the sunlight flickering through the trees. Frequently he took her down to the lake that was near the hospital, where they would sit on a small wooden bench by the water's edge. And though she was no longer able to enter into a canoe or small boat, Earl was able to wheel her onto a pontoon boat that was docked nearby, where they'd be in no hurry to get anywhere.

Of all the places where Earl noticed Ruth daydreaming, the water was where she did the most. Sometimes Earl was concerned that he'd lost her to daydreams and visions altogether, until she would gently turn her head and look at him with those ever-captivating eyes and sweet smile. And in those moments, Earl could feel his love for this woman grow.

But in the back of Earl's mind, he knew, all too painfully, that without a miracle these times of unexpected pleasure and peace would not endure. And though he never ceased praying for that miracle, it would never come. Sooner than he had hoped, he was at Ruth's hospital bedside one evening, fighting alongside his best friend for her life and silently preparing his heart, as best he could, to say goodbye. Her condition had sharply declined in recent days, and with their family surrounding them, including Earl's sister Stephanie who had traveled far to be with them, the doctor had delivered a prognosis that was not encouraging. She had lived longer than the doctors had predicted, though it now appeared that, despite all the prayers for healing, she was being called home, and called home quickly.

Ruth looked fondly at Earl and the surrounding family as her breathing grew heavier and more laborious, while her eyes began to grow heavy and become withdrawn. Earl leaned over and gently pressed his cheek against hers and whispered into her ear, "I love you, Ruth. I don't want you to leave yet . . . but if this is the end, know that I'll be coming for you as soon as I can."

At those words, Earl could feel her grip upon his hand tighten, though it was short-lived. In a way he would never forget, her hold on his hand slowly faded, and she breathed her last.

The room fell silent, with nothing to be heard but the faint sound of wind outside the windows. Earl slowly lifted his head from her cheek, his eyes still closed. Slowly, he opened them to see what his heart could not yet fully grasp. His girl, the love of his life, was gone.

"Goodbye, Ruth," he said with a quivering voice. Sniffles began to emerge from the room, and soon mourning. All the while, the wind outside continued to gently make its presence known.

Days later, on a cool autumn morning, people of all ages and backgrounds from Mountain, Cringle, and beyond were gathered together at the church for Ruth's funeral. Rarely had many of these residents seen so many people gather for a funeral, and few have been at one that seemed to evoke more joy and hope than gloom and despair. Life was in the air, and no one could escape it.

People talked and reminisced about old times until the sounds of piano filled the room and signaled the beginning of the funeral. After everyone was seated and the music came to a close, the pastor, who had been longtime friends with both Earl and Ruth, rose to speak.

"Today we celebrate a life well lived. Admittedly, I have used these words at many funerals; some of you have heard me do so. Today, though, when applying them to the life of Ruth Timmings, I say them with as much confidence as I ever have in all my years. From a young age, Ruth was one who graciously lived her days with others in mind, and did so all the way to the end.

"Ruth was a valiant wife; a constant support for her husband, who cherished her presence and placed great weight on her words. They exemplified teamwork in marriage and nurtured a fire in their relationship, centered around God, that grew in intensity as it matured, unlike so many that cool over time. I do not believe Earl would hesitate to admit that he would not be the man that he is, or accomplished all that he had, without Ruth at his side. And I believe her children, whom she so treasured, would say the same.

"And not only was she a valiant wife, but also an advocate and defender of the hurting and oppressed. From those widowed by the merciless war to those beset by chance circumstances of life or injustice, as well as those who were picking up the pieces after making poor choices they would go on to regret, Ruth was at their side to comfort. She was no enabler, but rather worked in tandem with the Almighty to comfort and restore.

"The book of Ecclesiastes challenges us to 'remember the day of death,' for one day we will all return to the ground from which we came. Mariners of old sailed with the words *memento mori*—a Latin phrase meaning "remember death," perhaps because they knew the dangers they faced when crossing the vast, untamed seas. The remembrance that death could come any day likely kept them prepared and alert.

"Like those mariners, we too travel down roads of such uncertainty, and no one here is guaranteed a tomorrow. No one. While many people run and hide from this truth all their days, only to find themselves staring it in the face unexpectedly, and unprepared, Ruth and her husband heeded these words in life and bore the fruits of doing so. They put their trust in One who conquered death once and for all, and were therefore able to stare it square in the face while living their lives to the fullest.

"Today, we are all saddened to have to say goodbye to one so special. Yet we can find joy unparalleled when considering where she now abides, and hold tightly to the treasure of her legacy. Today, friends, we truly celebrate a life well lived, and we ought to thank God for the time we had to share with her."

The man continued to speak for a short time, and after concluding his message, he invited others to come to the front and share how their lives were impacted by Ruth.

One by one, people came forward, and the stories they shared touched the hearts of everyone present. An old woman who was comforted by Ruth years ago when her husband had died in battle. A young man and middle-aged woman who had received gentle instruction from her in church, instruction that had cemented their faith. Two former patients she had treated with care and compassion while she was a nurse at the hospital. There were friends and neighbors, and later the pastor noted that he had never presided over a funeral in which so many eulogies were delivered. Regardless of how hard each person tried to remain composed, none of them could hold back tears as they told of their love for Ruth.

After the eulogies, the people traveled to the cabin and gathered down by the lake for the final portion of the service. Family and friends gathered on the shoreline, and silently watched as Earl walked slowly out onto the dock. Upon reaching the edge, he stopped and took a deep breath, then looked up at the blue skies and passing clouds where he said a silent thank you in his heart. He then looked down at the water, where the soft ripples and sounds of lapping water carried him back to a time where he and Ruth sat before these waters one Sunday afternoon.

"Earl, I think I've told you this before, but I'd like my ashes to be sprinkled over the lake."
Earl took a long look at her and swallowed hard, then mustered a crooked smile and leaned forward, taking her hand. "Okay, honey. That is what we'll do." Inside, however, the thought of her absence was still too powerful a thing for him to contend with. It wasn't a matter of denial but capacity.
"I don't want people to linger too long over a grave. I want them to be by the water, to be reminded

that I'm not in the ground but in heaven, fully alive, unhindered by age and decay. I want them to be reminded that life here is only a vapor, short and fleeting, and that there is true life in the water."

"Yes, Ruth, life is indeed in the water," he now whispered into the air, aware of the deeper spiritual implications she had been referring to. Deep things not above those of the common man, though leagues above and beyond the reach of the lofty, proud, and arrogant.

Slowly, he took the lid off of a smooth wooden urn, and then gently sprinkled the ashes over the water with the help of a slight breeze that carried them further out into the deep. After a moment of utter silence, he turned back to the audience on the shoreline and connected with every pair of eyes. Though he didn't know it, his moist eyes offered strength and compassion to their weary hearts.

"Remember, friends, where she is now, and nurture the memory of her life and how it impacted yours. Mourn, but only for a time, for she wouldn't want you crying for her too long. There is so much to live for; she would tell you that."

He then walked back to the shore, where his family embraced him. And he, along with many others in attendance, took one final look back at the waters before ascending the hill.

Earl, being at the rear of the procession, was the last one to look back, and his gaze turned out to be the longest. For at that moment, he was captured by the sight of an intensely bright white trail that emerged onto the water after a large cloud passed by, allowing a ray of sun to shine with all its strength onto the small ripples. The trail, so bright that it was hard to look at, spanned the entire lake, right up to the dock where Ruth's ashes were released into the air just moments ago.

"Thank you . . ." he said, too weary and overwhelmed to say or ponder anything more, then turned away to join his family.

Earl was buoyed by the support of his family in the days to come, though soon, in the quiet moments when all alone, the full weight of Ruth's passing would be felt. Pain and longing of an intensity previously unknown to him would send him to his knees in anguish, and he would feel engulfed in an utter darkness through which no light could break through.

While all his remaining days would be marked with a touch of sorrow caused by her absence, this great storm in his soul would eventually subside, and light would again pour into his life. Most days, he could be found before calm waters and setting sun, Jessie at his side, coffee in hand, and pen and journal ready to capture life, with gratitude for what was, what is, and what is to come.

A Gentle Breeze

Dear Ruth,

It has not been long since you spread your wings and flew away from us, and I miss you. I have not been able to pick up my pen for weeks. Even now, as I write this, it feels like a hundred pounds in my hand.

I can only imagine where you are at this moment, and though the thought brings me indescribable comfort, I still do not feel right without you beside me—as selfish as that may be. Seems life is one big ache with all kinds of stuff mixed in. Thankfully, a lot of good stuff. But the ache is strong and real right now without you here.

As you desired, your ashes have been spread over the lake. There was a gentle, steady breeze that day that carried them out into the deep. So many memories down there. So many sunsets and laughter and tears. There is no better place where they could have been scattered.

I went back down to the lake this morning for the first time since your funeral, just to sit and listen. Of course Jessie came with me, ever comforting, ever playful, and still doing great.

> *Recently, we've been going to the small lake over by my folks' old place, and every time I think about when I first got to know you there. The canoe rides, our talks on the bench. The present owners are so kind and urge me to come by whenever I want, and though I keep it to a minimum, I have shown up a handful of times. Keeps my memory strong, I believe, and usually turns into a time of heartfelt prayer, of giving thanks for such rich blessings and asking for strength of heart to keep on going in this life until my time is up. The temptation to resign still surfaces from time to time even at my age, and I cannot overcome it alone.*
>
> *I remember all the nights we sat out there before we were married, just drifting deeper and deeper in love, wooed by all the beauty that surrounded us. I can only count myself among the most fortunate men alive to have been able to experience the sweetness of falling for a girl like you. You could have had any man, Ruth, and you chose me. And I was made a better one because of you.*
>
> *I love you,*
> *Earl*

Earl folded the letter, which he had written on the dock weeks after her passing, and tucked it into his pocket. It was the last letter he ever wrote to Ruth, for he knew that he had to move on.

"Oh God, I miss her so much," he said aloud while looking desperately into the skies. "And right now, the pain from her absence and all these memories feels unbearable. I know there is the place waiting for me where no more hurt or sorrow exists, but right now that place seems far beyond sight." He paused and closed his eyes. With a deep sigh, and tears welling in his yes, his voice creaked forth again, half to God, half to himself, "I sometimes wonder if this is right to do—to go back and revisit all this year after year."

Earl rose from his chair and walked to the edge of the porch. Placing both hands on the rail to support himself, he leaned forward and bowed his head. Then, he began to weep.

"It sometimes gets so lonely here," he said between the tears. "So many of my friends have passed away, and the activity of life that is going on around me seems just out of reach. I once thought that when I'd be this age that I'd be stronger and more patient. But right now, I feel so weak and frail."

Just then, a strong gust of wind came along and brushed his face. It was followed by a gentle, enduring breeze that began to dry the tears from his cheeks. He lifted his head in the direction of the oncoming wind, and there in the distance was the eagle soaring high above the treetops.

"There you are, my friend," he said, half astonished at the sight. "Timely as ever."

He slowly reached into his pocket and pulled out the final timeworn letter.

Dear Earl,

If you are now reading this letter, it means that you have gone through all the letters and journals from our decades-long marriage. I hope your heart has been lifted, as mine was when compiling them.

Fifty years—can it really be? When we first started our journey together, the thought of spending so much time together seemed to be a fantasy; a stretch of time too large to grasp. Now, as I write, it seems to have been a blink, a fleeting gust of wind. A sweet-tasting, adventurous gust of wind that I'd go back and ride all over again if I could.

Thank you, Earl, my love. Thank you for being such a fine, loving husband to me; a tender, engaging father to our children; a winsome grandfather to our grandchildren; and a man of integrity and support to so many others. Thank you for showing us what a man can be who puts his Creator first in his life, and his family second above all else. Life comes from the river, as you often reminded us, and you remained in the river and hence led us faithfully through all these years that were filled with so many twists and turns, ups and downs.

Thank you for your unwavering support and encouragement in my nursing career, and for standing by my side through the many challenges it posed. Though I pulled away from it while raising the kids, you never let me forget how it was a part of me, and something I'd have to return to. It was a wonderful ability and asset to have that opened doors we couldn't have expected, like being a part-time nurse at our children's high school, creating an open door to engage them and their vast array of friends. It also opened the door for us to take trips into Central America, where the kids had such sweet, big smiles despite impoverished conditions. They melted you. They melted us. And it gave me the opportunity to tend to the needs of others right here in this hospital, where I am now receiving the same kind of care from other nurses and staff.

Thank you for keeping life exciting, whether a trip into the north or overseas, or something as simple as trying new coffee or a new trail through the woods, or even a night of dancing.

Thank you for holding on through the dry and discouraging seasons and for staying true to what you held dear even when times tempted you to pull back and retreat. And I know you were tempted, as all men are, to abandon your post. But you didn't.

Thank you for allowing me to walk with you through your doubts and fears, times when you wrestled with your humanity and the selfishness, weakness, nagging imperfections, and sometimes crippling insecurities that accompany it. Your humility in the presence of those villains made me respect you all the more, especially now in retrospect. Thank you for forging strong friendships with the men in your life who helped you walk through those seasons, who challenged and encouraged you, and who received the same from you.

Thank you for sitting at my side throughout this illness. So many times I would wake to see you sitting there, just looking at me, and then I'd feel warmth in my hand and notice that you were holding it, gently but firmly. I must admit, there were times when I woke first and just watched you while you were sleeping in the recliner next to me. Fifty years of waking up next to someone, seeing them breathing and at peace, and finding great delight in that—I still do now. And like Jessie, you are sometimes entertaining in your sleep, talking incoherently about such things as our friends scattered near and far, or even trout or bass that you must be catching down in the river. "Get it! It's a keeper!" you'd mumble, and then your arms and legs would start twitching. Oh, I can't help but laugh while thinking about it now. Once—and maybe I should keep this to myself, you uttered the words, "Don't take her yet, please . . . but your will be done." I don't recall my heart ever filling with sorrow as much as it did at that moment. And then I thought of the Father's love for us, and how it flowed through you, and all I could do is be overwhelmed in the stillness and utter silence of that hospital room.

I saw this love in the way you did your rounds in this hospital, stopping in the rooms of other patients who you have come to know during our time here. People who needed comfort and someone to hear them, to break the loneliness and sorrow, and help face the fear of imminent death. It was so thrilling to hear a few of the stories of how some responded to you telling them of the way that leads to that special place beyond the sun, and peace during their days here on earth. You showed them a reason for hope, even in what was likely the darkest hours of their lives.

I am sorry, Earl. I am so sorry if I am going to be the first to leave. I always imagined I'd be the one to remain after your passing, and for years I silently prepared myself for it. After all, women usually live longer than men. But a different plan seems to be in store for us, and though I would have written the script differently, I understand it is out of my hands.

I just reread the long letter you wrote me for our 50th wedding anniversary, and aside from saying that it made me cry rivers once again (like most of your letters), it reminded me of the road that waits at the end of this one, and how full and rich our lives were.

I don't want to die yet, Earl. I do not want to leave you and the family. Yet now, in this place, I feel a deep closeness to heaven that I have never felt before, and I cannot deny a feeling of excitement that comes with the thought of entering that place. I recall our conversations about how nearly impossible it is, with the exception of a few moments in life, to really grasp or conceive what passing through physical death into eternity must be like. Even though I still cannot fully grasp it, it does seem more touchable. More real. The only painful part about this is in knowing that you cannot share it with me; I don't believe anyone can who is not standing near the gates.

I haven't given up on God giving me more time, nor that he may choose to heal me altogether. I would never give up on the possibility of enjoying more years on earth, and know that I will not abandon that hope until it is retired in death. But as we have previously shared with each other, we know that in our hearts it doesn't seem to be the course that has been set, and it is with that gut feeling we shared that I set the tone of these words.

As death no longer holds ultimate power in our lives, so shall it be denied final power in this letter. Earl, child of God, man among men, son of Richard and Patricia, father of my children: I, your grateful wife and best friend, am crazy about you. Thank you for filling my life with so much color, for making my heart dance and growing old with me, for letting me ride with you.

I'll be waiting for you,
Ruth

Earl folded the letter and held it tightly in his hands, then stared off into the sky, his eyes moist but no longer shedding tears. He wondered if he was simply out of them, if his tear supply had been depleted, for within, his heart was moved beyond comprehension.

At that moment he knew what he had to do next. He placed the letter back into the shoebox, then looked over at

Jessie, who was snapping viciously at a jumbo fly that was buzzing around her head. Earl chuckled.

"C'mon, girl. We'll get that fly later. We have to go to the water now." Within seconds, she was following him down the steps and walking proudly beside him.

Earl reached the shoreline of the lake. It was so still and peaceful. He then walked to the end of the dock. He stood as straight as his old body could, a tree that had been battered by storms but still remained strong and rooted, and looked out across the waters.

"I miss you, Ruth. Your memory grows stronger within me each year when I read these letters, and in some strange way you grow even closer to me. You were, and remain, a treasure in my life. A treasure beyond compare. 'Why me?' I often wondered. Though I kept this from you, knowing that I should just be thankful, and that I'd get a swift, solid punch in the chest for asking." His voice had stopped trembling and broadcast strong and firm.

"Please know that I will not stop living, especially for others, so long as breath remains in my lungs. But regardless, I long to see you again, and cannot wait to ride with you in perfect oneness through eternity. I love you."

He then paused and looked into the water. It bore reflections of the sky, and prompted him to look up.

"God," he continued, "thank you for the gift of Ruth. I could not have asked for more. A part of me wishes you'd call me home too, but I'll remain here until you deem it's my time, doing what I can to make this a better place."

With Jessie sitting beside him, Earl remained at the edge of the dock for a moment longer. A great silence seemed to surround them. Earl stood with a steady, unwavering gaze fixed on the horizon that held so many visions of the past, present, and future. He could still feel the presence of pain in his heart, and knew that more was to come. Such was the way of life. Yet he found rest in the knowledge that joy and hope were stronger than any pain this world might hold.

And before he turned around to return to the cabin, a breeze began to blow over the surface of the lake, causing ripples to spread across the deep. Comforted, Earl gently placed his hand on Jessie's head and breathed deeply. "We're not alone, friend."

Following is an excerpt from
Rearview Sunset
by Brett Champan

A Splash in the Water

August 25, 2006, early Saturday morning

Dreams are mysterious things. This I have always believed and know to be true. Some are nothing more than the residue of the day's thoughts or worries that have been taunting the soul. Others are something far greater, sometimes discernible, other times revealing deep things that are often too wonderful for the recipient to fully grasp in the present time.

And then there are some that appear to be a combination of the two, like the one I had just moments ago on this cool August night. It was so lucid and detailed, so much so that it has taken what seems to be minutes after waking for me to regain my senses and realize that I am in bed in our northern Wisconsin cabin, right where I had gone to sleep hours earlier.

Coming out of the dream, I shot up from my pillow into sitting position, beads of sweat dripping from my forehead, a deep breath escaping from my body as if it had been locked up for years. Other than the moonlight gently pouring in through the skylight, all is dark, still, and silent. Within me, though, there is little silence. Rather, a subtle angst roars from the deep, one that has been brewing for a time. I have little doubt that this angst influenced the dream, and I replay it over and over in these fleeting moments while sitting here, pondering its significance.

In the dream we were sailing over the Atlantic, cutting steadily forward through the large, gentle swells. I can still taste the sweet air as we moved up and down and can hear the hoarse sound of our fiery British captain's voice,

"Men, do not forget these times."

Then came the mounting tension that steadily grew as a mighty storm rushed in. For hours we fought it, our captain maintaining a proper air of reverence and confidence that fueled his crew's hope for safe passage through the writhing ocean. I can still feel the salt water splashing my face, and more than anything, I recall the burning desire to survive in order to reach the shores of North America, where the heart of a beautiful young woman hung in the balance, awaiting my return. Despite the danger and lack of control over the situation, a sturdy peace existed within me that said I would see her again. "Not yet," I said while looking into the sky through the pouring rain. "*Not yet.*"

The dream didn't end there. Like a mist, I was taken from the small vessel into a forest where I ran with all my heart, dodging trees and jumping through puddles and over fallen logs, a sense of something ominous and dark lurking. I had to swerve to avoid hissing snakes and low-hanging branches, which appeared more like bony hands and fingers reaching out to harm me. I lashed out at them, pushing them away, but there were so many. I remember sunlight bursting through the trees, which took my eyes off them and filled me with hope and strength to keep running.

I eventually reached a trail, where a powerful, good-natured horse was awaiting my arrival. In a way that can only happen in a dream, I was whisked up onto the saddle and began galloping faster than the wind down a well-trodden trail of soft earth, thunderous sounds rising from below as the hooves mercilessly beat the ground. Looking back once, I could see a trail of dust left in our wake. We rode for what seemed to be hours, the wind whipping me in the face as the horse cut swiftly through the trail.

> The ride eventually took us into the night, where a touch of moonlight lit the trail and brought the shadows of the trees to life. The steed pressed on, his eyes able to penetrate the darkness, of which he had no fear. I just held on, feeling alive in every part of my being.
>
> With the emergence of dawn, we finally came to the shoreline of a small lake. I dismounted and peered across the water. There, standing alone on the opposite shoreline, was a beautiful young woman with long, dark, flowing hair looking sullenly down at the ground to her side, as if a fire in her heart had been extinguished. Her face was not foreign to me.
>
> I plunged into the lake at the sight of her. I swam towards the beauty with long, hard strokes, and after emerging from the water and rushing to where she stood, I reached out to take her hand and was met with a radiant, blinding white light.
>
> And then I woke.

Beau closed his journal, blinked hard, and turned off the small bedside lamp on his right before lying back down. He then turned his head to the right and reached over again to take hold of the alarm clock. He pressed the light button—3:45 a.m. After giving his mind a few more seconds to grasp what time it really was, he let out another deep breath and shook his head to clear his mind.

Drawn by the moonlight and a pull on his heart to go outside in hopes of finding rest for the soul, he quietly slipped out of bed and put his robe and slippers on. He walked like a feather out of the room and down the hall toward the spiral stairs, just past the room where his two children slept. Along the way, he stopped outside their barely cracked door and put his ear up close. Sounds of quiet breathing could be heard from within. Comforted by this, and still only half awake, he continued onward to the stairs and descended to the first floor. He crept to the front door, traded slippers for outdoor shoes, and slowly turned the door handle so as to not wake anyone.

Yet not everyone would remain asleep, despite his stealth movements. Highway, their trusty yellow Labrador, lifted his head and began to wag his tail. He whined just loud enough for Beau to hear and released a big yawn that stretched his jaw to near-breaking point.

"You stay here, okay buddy? I need to go out alone for a little while." It seemed the dog understood, for down went his head, resting his chin onto his paws in a sad-like fashion that tugged at Beau's heart. His tail continued to wag, though, just enough to make it known that his master could still change his mind and ask him to come with.

"Not this time, Highway. We'll be together out there on the water soon enough."

He exited the front door and walked down toward the dock with a brisk pace. It was a cool night, typical of the season. Upon reaching the dock, he stepped onto the solid wood boards and looked into the moonlit sky, which caused the water to glisten wildly. Inside, he was struggling with all the thoughts and energy running through his mind, body, and soul.

"In order to move forward, one must first look back." These words, as they often had in recent times, entered his mind. They were quoted by a pastor at the funeral of an old friend who had passed away a few weeks earlier. He was a noble man of great character who lived a simple but fulfilling life marked by an equally simple but powerful faith, and as a result, had accumulated great honor and many stories that had left a legacy for his children, grandchildren, and beyond. It was for his family and others that he lived, and he had impacted a great number of people along the way. He was much like a man that Beau had known years ago, a man whose life left an indelible mark on him.

The words at his funeral moved Beau to act on a desire that had previously been planted in him. Though still very young by most standards, he felt it was time to take a closer look into his own journey, well aware that each day could be his last and believing that, in some way, it would benefit those close to him. And perhaps he had more reason to feel this way than the common man. Just a year earlier, he sat in a hospital room, where his doctor gently informed him of a liver condition, fraught with uncertainties as to origin and nature, which would likely take his life in one year's time. He swallowed hard upon hearing those words, unsure of what emotions to display or even what he was feeling at that moment. Thoughts of every conceivable aspect of life flashed through his mind.

One year had now passed, however, and in a way that his doctor and his staff could not and cannot explain, the condition had subsided. For now, he lived, more so than ever. He hoped, God willing, that many more adventures and experiences might find him, though he was ever aware that the number of his days was out of his hands. He might have influence over the relevance of them but not the duration.

Now he stood out on the dock, the dream that led him down there still moving through his mind: the voyage over the sea, running and galloping on the horse through the woods, reaching out to the beautiful girl—just a few glimpses into the story that led him to this day. A story comprised of many stories that all seemed to piece together and stretch far beyond happenstance. A story that was just one small but significant piece of an even greater tale, one that travels beyond past, present, and future.

Part of this small story included an old, wise man who lived not long ago, who Beau called a great friend. There was also a host of others, including a beautiful young woman and what may have been angels, who helped him find his way home after he had wandered far from it—farther than he knew. Some of those faces he knew he would never see again, except perhaps in heaven. Others he hoped he might see one day, though something told him that they were sent across his path only for a time, not to be seen again for a long time, if ever. Of this he could not be certain, and therefore, he believed it warranted no further pondering, though of course he did sometimes anyway.

What he did know was that they helped him find life, saved him from certain death. They were instruments that led him through dreadful darkness, where all vision and hope was obscured, if not completely absent, to an unexpected destiny and true love that rocked his soul. And even when he later encountered death and pain via the departure of one who meant so much to him, even there he found life and joy in its purest form. He would learn that pain is sometimes one of the surest signs of life.

He would never forget those people and times that carried him across the highways of the Midwest and beyond. For that he was forever grateful, forever shaped, forever changed. And the best part was that so much lay ahead, whether in this life or the next.

So now he was left with the task of illuminating his piece of the great tale, the people and places that decorated it and made it what it is. Though he wouldn't right out say that God told him to do this, he did feel divine approval was on his side, just like when King David's servant told him to go and do whatever he had in mind, for God would be with him.

Yet of this task he was now in angst, not really sure where to begin or understanding some of the emotions running through him. It wasn't the first time he looked back, though he was going deeper this time, and there was so much. And he knew it would not come without challenge. Though he loved depth in life and was no stranger to solitude, which would be plentiful, part of him moaned at the thought of it. Men can achieve great feats and risk much in life, but to step out into the silence to unearth the deep places of the heart for oneself and others to see is perhaps one of the greatest challenges. Who knows what one may find down there.

To dig up old memories is to invite both the joy and pain in life, and that was exactly where Beau was heading. Some memories produce laughter and warmth, others result in sorrow and tears. But in the end, it can lead to greater freedom, both for the individual and those in his life. It was for this freedom he pressed onward.

Opposition and its ally, darkness, would accompany the process as well. All good things face evil resistance. Darkness hates light; it's always running away from it, always trying to keep people from it.

"There is just so much!" he growled under his breath with a reverent ferocity into the sky, breaking the silence. He couldn't help but pace back and forth on the dock, unfettered by the howls and other sounds of the night that surrounded him, somewhat surprised by these emotions. His eyes, which burned in the crisp air, traveled to the ground and then back up to the heavens. As he often did when on his feet, he prayed aloud, with an ever-increasing and confident tone with a few pauses in between, hands and arms swinging and flailing about at times to add exclamation to his words.

"I know I need to look back and share this story… all the stories. But where do I begin; how do I pull it all together?" His breathing became heavier, intensity rising. "And I cannot do this alone. I will not do this alone." He continued to pace around, various combinations of thoughts coming out of his mouth that could not find their way into complete sentences. Frustration mounted.

"And Highway doesn't count!"

Just then, right as he was about to implode into the early morning and become a memory to all who knew him, a swift, explosive splash took place just feet from the edge of the dock from where he stood. "Whoosh!" With a slight gasp, his body jolted, and he was shaken loose from his previous train of thought. He looked down toward the commotion and saw the end of a muskrat's tail go swirling into the depths in the direction of the dock. After a few moments of silence passed, he could hear the animal settle right below the wood boards under his feet. Sounds of rustling came from underneath, as if the little critter was snuggling up to bed, uneasy that this large, uninvited guest stood above his resting place.

Soothed in a way he couldn't understand right then and there, he stopped pacing. His arms fell down to his sides, and he just looked forward into the moonlit lake and the dark shadow of treetops that lined the horizon, then up into the starry sky. Peace settled over him, one like a river that breaks through an old dam and sweeps through a small village, removing debris and old branches as it flows.

"Okay," he humbly whispered into the air. The words left his mouth. He felt lighter. His eyes and mouth closed in concession to the powerful silence that was all around him. His head lowered, and he slowly turned to return to the cabin, exhausted but relieved.

Beau slipped into bed as quietly as possible. Just before his eyes surrendered and were about to close, his wife turned over and nestled up to him, putting her left arm on his chest and resting her open palm just below his neck.

"Honey," she said softly in a dreamy tone that made him wonder if she was talking in her sleep. He could feel her warmth on his skin.

"Yeah?" he responded, opening his eyes to the sound of her voice, somewhat surprised that she had awoken.

"It's going to be okay. You'll be given the strength and help you need to travel back there." A small sigh came out of him upon hearing this, and he was about to speak. Sensing this, she placed the tip of her finger over his lips to stop any unnecessary words. *"Sleep honey, sleep,"* her voice trailed off. As quickly as she awoke, she returned to slumber. Beau often marveled at her ability to do this, as he was now.

Her words settled on him like a feather, gentle yet poignant. As if drugged, his eyes closed, and he drifted away into a deep, fitful sleep.

The Canoe

It wasn't long before Beau awoke for the second time. The moonlight had now passed and was replaced by the splendor of the morning light, which crept slowly through the window on the eastern wall of the bedroom to rest upon the foot of the bed. All was silent.

Lying on his back, he heard the soft breathing of his wife and turned his head to look at her. She lay sound asleep with her hand on his arm, peaceful as could be.

He then turned to his right to check the clock: 5:55 a.m. Looking back toward the ceiling, he realized that the angst that had come and gone earlier in the morning was replaced by a great peace and eagerness to face the day, much to his satisfaction.

As the sun made its way over the distance of the bed and shone on them like a warm ray from heaven, it invited him to come outside and join in the celebration of a new day. He loved the early morning hour, and though his mind and body were eager to venture out for a quick taste of air before breakfast, he wanted to be there when his wife awoke to see her soft hazel eyes open and her morning smile that made him forget what time of day it was. With or without makeup and brushed hair, she captivated him and became more beautiful to him with each passing season.

As he lay on his back with the covers up to his neck, he resolved to get up and head outside, knowing that he could easily return to bed before she woke. Just at that moment, however, he could feel her body begin to squirm ever so slightly, and with one fluid motion, she rolled over into him, snuggling her body close and nestling her head below his chin. Her soft whimpers and calm breaths were now so close and overpowering to his senses that he knew he was not going anywhere right then and there.

After settling, her eyes opened briefly and met his. She smiled coyly before giving him a soft kiss that was followed by her return to dreaming. He again marveled at the way she was able to fall asleep, as if there was a switch to turn on and off. This even made him a bit envious, since sleep often came with greater effort for himself.

Sensing it was a fitting time to sneak out, he gently brushed her hair aside, kissed her on the forehead, and made his way out from under the covers. He set his feet upon the cool hardwood floor, which sent a shiver up his spine. After putting on a worn pair of jeans, a white cotton T-shirt, and his worn blue and grey checkered flannel that hung on a small brass hook on the closet door, he grabbed his journal from the nightstand and quietly walked to the door and opened it, taking one final glance back at her before closing it behind him.

On his way down the hallway to the stairs, he again stopped to check on the kids but this time slowly opened the door to look in. Like a brilliant sunset, the sight of them often made him lose track of whatever was previously on his mind and stand in reverence, as if it was the first time he had looked upon them. They were sound asleep with rustled hair and mouths agape, with no sign of life other than the rise and fall of the sheets that covered their bodies, evidence that life in the form of air was passing through them. A small dabble of drool dripped slowly down the side of young Wade's mouth, providing reassuring evidence as well.

As he stood there, motionless, fresh memories and thoughts of their futures passed through his mind. Looking upon these little ones, upon his family as a whole, was one of the greatest reminders of why he woke each day. "All men die, but few men really live." The time-tested quote from one of his favorite movies came to mind, as it often did, reminding him that a man is dead unless living for something greater than himself: for others. He slowly closed the door once again and made his way to the stairs and to the front door that allowed him access to all the wonders of the morning.

"Ah, Highway, my faithful comrade of the early hour. Now we can go out together." Few times, if ever, had his trusty yellow Labrador not been awake to greet his master, yearning inside and wagging his tail with sweet anticipation for their morning venture, especially when up at the cabin. Beau walked over to his hairy friend, rustled him up, and then allowed the beast to show some affection in the form of lapping his tongue over his face in a way that most people find offensive, including his wife.

"Honey, he licks himself in certain areas, you know," she would say with a slight grimace on her face while sipping her coffee.
"My lady, this dog offers unconditional love. The least I can do is allow him to bond with me in one of the few ways he knows how."

The discussion usually ended with his wife emerging victoriously, unfairly using threats of withholding her own forms of affection if he kept it up. "Marriage and dogs . . . never an easy balance," he thought.

After the bonding had ended, the two proceeded to walk the sloped path to the lake below. Down a steep incline on the other side of the cabin they could hear the lush sounds of the river. Often the challenging decision of which body of water to go to presented itself, though this morning the lake won out, for on its shores sat the canoe that they would soon set out on. He wanted to give it a quick inspection before packing it and departing.

Upon coming to the shoreline, Beau looked out over the expanse and took a deep breath, inhaling the cool, invigorating air. A thick fog hovered over the water, so much so that he could not see more than twenty feet across it. The two then walked over to the canoe, and Beau looked it over, tipping it on its side to let the water from the previous day's rain drain out.

On many mornings while at the cabin, they would start the day paddling along the glassy water. There were few better ways to embrace the dawn. One of those ways was when his wife and kids rose early enough to join them, all piling into the craft. The odds of tipping improved, though Beau believed some risk was good for their souls and therefore welcomed the opportunity.

Though Beau knew God gave neither spirit nor soul to anything made of aluminum or wood or any other kind of material, he felt there was something special about this one. Perhaps it was the wooden oars that had been through so much or the memories he had of sharing time fishing in it with an old friend of the family, who once owned it.

Most likely, though, it was the memory of a very special time in it under the setting sun not too many years ago, one that would never be forgotten.

Beau sat down on the craft and opened his small, black leatherbound journal to a fresh page and took a pen from the chest pocket of his flannel. After a few moments, he began to pen some words while continuing to admire his surroundings that never failed to inspire.

> *Later Saturday morn, lakeside*
>
> There are few things in life that renew the soul and perspective as much as unhurried time away with loved ones. Those things, which on some lesser days present themselves as burdens and responsibilities, oft taken for granted, now appear as rich blessings and gifts that deserve everything I have to give.
>
> I can hear the trees, water, and wind up here, and they all speak of the past, present, and future. It is time to look back. As a wise old friend once told me, stories are meant to be shared, especially ones that reach into the hearts of others.
>
> The dream still lingers in my mind. Unlike most other dreams, its contents still remain clear to me—pieces of the past that I had forgotten, lost sight of somewhere along the way, until recent times, which have been bringing them back to light.
>
> I trust more will come as I venture out to listen.

He closed the journal, called out to Highway, who was now patrolling the shoreline, and together they walked back to the cabin. Before ascending the steps, Beau stopped at the woodshed that sat just behind the cabin and took hold of the time-tested maul to split firewood for the coming winter. He positioned several logs and unleashed on them, swinging the instrument with precision and power. Living in the city, he rarely had the opportunity to use it and cherished the moment.

Often, he wished he could be a farmer, if for nothing else than to enjoy the manual labor in the morning hour that quickened the spirit.

After splitting the final log, he set the maul aside, stacked the cut pieces in the shed and gathered some dry firewood to carry inside. He was hoping his wife would still be in bed so that he could have a fire ready for her. It was still summertime, though the morning was brisk and fitting for the sight and sounds of a living, crackling fire. She was already up, though, and the excellent smell of freshly brewed coffee was lingering heavily in the air, stirring the senses.

While knelt before the fireplace, Beau crinkled a few pieces of old newspaper, set them under the grate, then placed small pieces of kindling and a couple larger logs on top of them. He pulled a strike-anywhere match from a small box and ignited it by flicking it off of his top front teeth. It was a trick he learned as a kid and never let go of, and the taste of sulfur in his mouth afterward would never let go of him.

After lighting the paper, he repositioned himself, sitting back far enough to stretch out his legs while keeping an eye on the fire to make sure it grew to maturity. Other than occasionally poking and prodding the wood, he sat there, motionless, gazing into the flame.

"Is it all good and safe out there, hun?" asked his wife with a playful yet ladylike tone as she came up behind him, bending over slightly to wrap her arms around him and kiss him softly on both cheeks. "Sure is, my lady," he replied, shaking any dust off his hands before gently reaching behind him to grab a hold of her and pull her over his shoulders. She wasn't sure what he was trying to do but was relieved to find herself safe in his lap when the process was over, where she received a return kiss or two.

Soon their coffee cups were in hand, the delicate wisps of steam rising above the rim. They talked of this and that and the coming week that they would be spending apart; while Beau and Highway would be away, she and the kids would be volunteering at Whispering Pines camp just three miles up the road, a place that for years had been a part of their lives. Pleasantness surrounded their talk, which revealed a depth and transparency in their relationship that came from weathering the many challenges inherent in marriage, even one as young as theirs. Soon they were joined by the kids, who came strolling down the stairs, rubbing their sleepy eyes, drawn by the anticipation of hugs and breakfast.

With the clock ticking, breakfast was prepared, and they sat down to eat, taking hands in prayer. Though Beau usually led the family this way, Alyssa volunteered and brought smiles to her parents when hearing her sweet five-year-old voice saying thank you for Mommy and Daddy and Wade and Highway and Mommy's cooking and the water and trees and especially for the bright morning star.

"Amen."

After breakfast, Beau, with little three-year-old Wade's assistance, helped clear off the table and afterward went for a short walk outside while Mom and Alyssa did the dishes. Most of the time, Wade held his father's hand as they walked around the yard, his eyes shooting to and fro with wild excitement and curiosity into the forest and everywhere else. At one point he released his grip to bend down and pick up a small fallen branch that he proceeded to wield like a sword, hitting his father right on the kneecap with one of the strokes.

"That's my boy," said Beau with a proud, slight grimace, pleased to see the young warrior revealed in the child. He knew this was only a taste, though, and that it would be years before his son would have to pick up and carry a real sword.

By most standards their marriage was still young, their role as parents younger still. New experiences presented themselves each day, challenges that required new strategies amidst days that moved so fast that they often hesitated to blink for concern they might miss something in the kids and in each other. More often than not, it seemed like they were just hanging on for dear life, with many prayers and occasional phone calls for direction to those further along in parenting. Somewhere along the journey, a greater appreciation for their imperfect parents emerged too.

Beau loaded the minivan with his family's luggage and helped them settle in. "Bye, Daddy!" shouted both Alyssa and Wade from the backseat. Wade looked especially sad that his pa wasn't coming with.

"Son, you listen to your mother while I'm away, and protect your sister, okay?" He looked up at his dad, a proud smile coming over his face.

"Okay."

"Be careful, Beau. I want to see you in one piece when you return. I'll be waiting for you." She looked at him longingly, and they exchanged a kiss and a hug before she climbed in the van.

"Beau," she said through the window before driving off, "I thought you might want these." She handed him some note cards with writing on them. "I thought they might provide you with some light on cloudy days." With that, she ran her fingers through his hair and drove off down the gravel driveway and onto the road.

Beau looked at the cards, then put them in his flannel pocket and buttoned it, as if safeguarding a valuable jewel. As soon as the van was out of sight, he wished it was returning. Yet the time had come to go, and he took a deep breath and went to load the canoe with supplies for the week and lock up the cabin before setting out.

While walking along with Highway, he felt a strange deterrent as he approached the cabin. It was as if a whisper was telling him not to go. He was not unfamiliar with this kind of whisper, the kind that produces an uneasy feeling inside. Lifting his head to look at the sky, he kept walking and in doing so recalled the words that came down through Solomon, a king of old—words that whispered a different message.

"Let your eyes look straight ahead, fix your gaze directly before you."

That whisper he trusted, and he clung to it while his pace increased.

Beau and Highway climbed into the canoe and pushed off into the still lake. By now the sun had risen above the treetops in the eastern horizon and was shining brightly over all the land, slightly filtered by some scattered clouds. The wind was soft and mild, and he could feel it move across his face and through his hair, sending him into frequent daydreams that grew more and more vivid. Highway sat calmly in the front of the canoe, exempted from paddling and given lookout duty, staring intently into the distance, into the water and sky, mesmerized in the same way as his master by the majesty of the glassy water and thin, dispersing fog that hovered slightly above it.

"I wonder what that dog is thinking of," Beau would often wonder.

They paddled on into the distance, sending soft ripples into the lake on both sides of their small, fully loaded vessel. The shoreline of the cabin soon became a distant memory. Daydreams began to run more rampant as the beauty of creation surrounded them—thoughts of the joys and challenges of being a husband and father, friendships, parents and siblings and other acquaintances, the wonderful journey and all its twists and turns that led him to this point in his life, the unknown adventure that lay before him in the days and years to come.

"All gifts," he reminded himself as often as necessary. "All gifts." With broad, heavy strokes, the canoe lunged forward. Once in a while, the two males would exchange looks, sharing conversation in their respective ways. Beau usually did most of the talking, though sometimes Highway would respond with a few low-volume sounds that fell between a bark and a howl.

After a half hour, Beau began to paddle more leisurely, realizing that he had better conserve some energy. It would take several hours, including a portage or two, in order to reach the small island that would be their fortress for the week. With one slow, smooth stroke, he looked down into the waters and up into the sky to see all the different shapes and pictures of clouds, all of which pointed to something bigger. In the haste of life, he often lost sight of this, of how the clouds and stars and moon and sun are evidence that there is more to life than his schedule.

At one point Beau ceased paddling and looked over the edge of the canoe. He could see clearly his reflection looking back at him through the gentle ripples sent from the craft. As he followed them until they were no more, he was taken back to times as a child when he would look into those deep, mysterious waters.

Times that seemed so innocent, when so much remained to be shaped.

6/16

Independence Public Library
23688 ADAMS STREET • P.O. BOX 99
INDEPENDENCE, WI 54747
PHONE 715-985-3616